# Before The Dawn

(Book 2 in *The Grayson Trilogy*)

# GEORGIA ROSE

2nd Edition Published by Three Shires Publishing

ISBN: 978-0-9933318-3-1 (paperback)

ISBN: 978-0-9933318-4-8 (ebook)

www.georgiarosebooks.com

Cover design by the team at SilverWood Books (www.silverwoodbooks.co.uk)

British Library Cataloguing in Publication Data

A CIP catalogue record for this book is available from the British Library.

## <u>The Grayson Trilogy</u>

A Single Step

Before The Dawn

Thicker Than Water

This book is dedicated to Katherine and Patrick –
thank you, I couldn't have wished for better people.

# A Note from the Author

To all you lovely people who have kindly chosen this book to read please note, if you haven't already, that this is the second book in a Trilogy. I strongly advise you to read *A Single Step*, which is the first one, before you get stuck into this. While *Before the Dawn* is a complete story in itself I will not be rehashing a lot of back story from *A Single Step* and you will be missing many of the reasons why characters are where they are or behave as they do. If you think this is a blatant attempt by an author to sell more of their earlier book – well perhaps it is...*but* if you go to find *A Single Step*, and find it is not at a price that encourages you to buy it please contact me (details at the back of this book) and I will be delighted to get a copy to you. I only want you to get the best experience of reading *Before the Dawn* that you can.

Thank you

Georgia

"We gain strength, and courage, and confidence by each experience in which we really stop to look fear in the face…we must do that which we think we cannot."

Eleanor Roosevelt

# Chapter 1

He'd been gone a week. Once I hadn't wanted him around me, now I longed for his return. Strange how things could change, I mused, as I brought the ponies in from the field. Zodiac waited patiently as I turned to close the gate while Benjy cheekily nosed his way into my jacket pocket, searching for treats. I smiled ruefully. The feelings I'd had towards Trent bordered on dislike when I'd first met him more than a year ago. Time and events had changed everything.

It was a cool Sunday evening in early July. The day had consisted of showers interspersed with sunny highlights but not much by way of heat. I finished my yard duties, checked that the horses, Regan and Monty, were settled in their stables, then went over to the cottage.

After showering, a text arrived as I dressed. From Cavendish. It was marked URGENT and asked me to come to the Manor at 20.00 hours for a meeting. A thought flickered through my mind. Just me? Should I be worried? This was an unusual request. Then I realised...if Cavendish was here...? That thought was answered instantly as my phone rang.

"You're back?" I felt my pulse rise with the anticipation of hearing him.

"I'm back." Trent's voice, rich, deep and instantly soothing. "Have you received a text?"

"Yes, what's going on?"

"You'll find out soon enough...I was hoping to see you before the meeting, though – any chance you could get here a bit earlier?"

"I'm leaving now."

"I'm going to jump in the shower, so come to my apartment."

"Okay." Ending the call, I grabbed my keys and left, saying goodbye to Susie who was already curling herself up in her bed as I pulled the door closed behind me.

I drove the pickup to the courtyard at the back of the Manor and parked opposite the door to the gym. I ran up to his front door, knocking on it loudly. It opened immediately and he grabbed my hand, drawing me towards him, hugging me tightly as I wrapped my arms around his still-damp body and breathed him in. I pulled back a little to take a better look, my fingers touching the light covering of dark hair on his chest that tapered as it travelled down the taut line of his stomach before disappearing into the towel slung low around his waist. But I had no chance to say anything as his hands moved up to my face, tilting it towards him. His lips touched mine softly, and as they did I heard him groan and desire overwhelmed us.

Making it out of the entrance hall, I lay in his bed sometime later, gazing at him as our breathing steadied.

"I do love a good homecoming," he said, grinning back at me.

"What happened?" Trent made out he didn't know what I was talking about. I indicated the bruising starting to blacken his eye, the similar discoloration down the sides of his ribs.

"Ah...we ran into a bit of resistance," he admitted. I pulled a face at his understatement and he smiled. "Don't worry, Cavendish looks much worse than this." As if that was somehow meant to make me feel better.

2

He leant over and kissed the soft pink skin that covered the wound on my shoulder. "How's this doing?"

I shrugged off his concern. "It's fine, getting better every day."

"Good." Trent looked at his watch. "Come on, we'd better not be late." He leapt up and started to dress.

"So what's going on?" I asked as nonchalantly as I could, trying to cover the anxiety I felt at being called into a meeting. I was wiggling my way back into my jeans as he paused, then said, "Trouble is heading our way."

A short while later we walked into Cavendish's office to find many of the staff from the estate already there. So not just me then, I thought with relief as Trent leant closer and murmured, "Try not to be too angry with me." Grinning, he let go of my hand and indicated I should sit down on one of the settees where most of the others were already seated. He went on walking up to the desk where Cavendish was standing, greeting people as he went.

I'd been working at the Melton Manor Estate, owned by Lord and Lady Henry Cavendish, as the stable manager for over a year now. As far as the outside world and, until recently, I was concerned the Melton Estate was a family home and productive agricultural enterprise with a staff of around thirty. Although I'd been aware that Cavendish and Trent carried out some sort of work off the estate, it had only been recently, since Trent and I had got together a few weeks ago, that I'd found out the estate actually provided an external force for the Secret Intelligence Services, SIS, or what I knew as MI6, to call upon. And I was already pretty certain that this meeting was not going to be about estate business.

I squeezed in next to Clare Greene who was tying her long blonde hair into a loose plait. As she moved up to let me in she asked if I knew what was going on. I met her inquisitive hazel eyes and shook my head. I was as mystified as she was. I saw her boyfriend, Will Carlton, and the other boys standing in a group a little further away, talking. As I looked from them towards the desk at the far end of the room I noticed a smartly dressed woman wearing a fitted suit, her platinum blonde hair in a severe but stylish bob. She wore dark-rimmed glasses which intensified her rather intimidating look. She reminded me of a bird of prey, possibly a hawk, and I didn't need to be told who she was. Sharpe. At long last I could put a face to the name. She was Cavendish's personal assistant and, despite liaising with me by email when I'd joined the staff, she was the one person who worked here that I'd never met.

Greene and I chatted for a few minutes, along with everyone else, the level of noise increasing as the rest of the staff joined us. Anticipation was growing in the room, and I could see the eagerness on some faces that were keen, like me, to find out what was going on.

Someone banged on the desk and silence fell immediately. All heads turned in that direction, ready to listen.

"Good evening," Cavendish began. "Thank you all for coming at such short notice. I'm going to hand over to Trent for a moment to bring you up to speed with the problem we're facing, and then I'll speak further on what action we need to take."

Trent stepped forward, looking calm, controlled and confident. I was suddenly aware of how little I knew about him, or about what he did, never having seen him in what appeared to be his familiar territory. He instantly commanded everyone's attention, and by their silence it seemed he had their respect also.

"As you all know to some degree or other, through the work we've done with SIS we've been brought in to stop the illegal activities of an organisation that has a vast operational network. This organisation originated in

4

Russia, but has now spread throughout all the post-Soviet states. Until recently its activities had been restricted to the same area, but it's now turned its attention to Britain, along with some other western European countries, and although this is not the usual fodder SIS deal with this threat from overseas can no longer be ignored, which is why we've become involved. To date this involvement has consisted mostly of research, both here as well as some work in the field as we build up a picture of what we're up against.

"In short, the organisation deals in drug and human trafficking, prostitution, kidnapping and extortion. It also supports terrorism by supplying arms to anyone who has the money to buy them. You name it – if they can make money from it, they will do it.

"The organisation is headed by the Polzin family, which is led by several brothers, all of whom have a ruthless reputation. They have large numbers of equally brutal people working for them. Some of them we've come up against before so we have an idea of what we're dealing with. More details will follow at future briefings, but as a warning, if their own people step out of line they are dealt with harshly, so you can imagine what they do to their enemies. I don't want anyone to be under any illusion as to what we're facing." He paused, his jaw clenched as he looked round, energy emanating from him. The silence was complete; as if under a spell the whole room held its collective breath. Then he broke the tension, smiled across at Cavendish, and I let my own breath go as he continued.

"Now...despite our current appearance..." He hesitated as laughter broke out, and raised his hand to quell the joshing from the boys. I'd noticed Cavendish was also sporting a black eye, although his bruising extended down his cheek where the skin was broken and his lip split. The room quietened again as Trent continued, "...Cavendish and I have recently had some success, but in the process have ruffled a few feathers. We've broken up their network of human trafficking into this country, which has had a knock-on impact for their prostitution business as well. It's a start, but there's much more for us to do. We're working on that, and this is likely to involve more of you coming with us." I glanced over at the group of boys who appeared to be relishing the prospect, then turned back as Trent was speaking again.

"However, the reason we've called you all here is that it seems the Polzin family haven't taken our interference well, and not being the sort of people to take such setbacks lying down they appear to be intent on retaliation. Through the intelligence-gathering resources at MI6 there has been a credible threat identified as coming from this group, specifically targeted against Cavendish." A low murmur rose through the room, silenced swiftly as Trent spoke again.

"It's our understanding that because of his high profile this organisation is targeting him as a kidnap prospect with a view to extorting money from our government, as well as obviously disrupting our efforts against them." Looks of concern grew on the faces of those around me, and at that moment I spotted Grace, Lady Cavendish, who had crept in late and was now perched on a chair next to Mrs F, the cook. Not surprisingly, she looked anxious.

Trent glanced around the room again before he went on. "This is only an initial briefing, and I'm going to hand back to Cavendish shortly, but before I do, I want to be very clear. This type of situation is the reason why we've all been brought together. This is what we've planned for, this is what we've trained for and it is our expectation that you will support us in the actions we're going to be taking." He stepped back to a murmur of approval and spontaneous applause, but ignoring that he looked directly across the office and locked his gaze on to mine. I gave him a small smile. I hoped he'd find it a reassuring one, for although I felt a little shaken at what I'd heard, I was also full of pride for him, and Cavendish, for what they were involved in; for what they'd already achieved. I'd had no idea, and could understand why Trent thought I might be angry with him. Leaving me in the dark about his activities was his idea of protecting me.

Cavendish, who clutched a clipboard in one hand, silenced the room again as he started, his delivery more laid-back than Trent's had been.

"Okay, so Trent's filled you in with an overview of what we're dealing with. Can I say at the outset, despite what Trent has just said, if there is anyone who doesn't want to be involved in what we're planning in any way, they only have to say. It won't be a problem." He paused allowing his words to sink in, giving people an out if they wanted one. Judging by my perception of the feeling in the room I doubted anyone would take it.

Cavendish went on: "Right, we believe it's likely that if an attack is made against me it will be made here. This would be the easiest place for them to get to me. When I'm away from here I'll have Trent with me, plus possibly some others among you, so I feel I'll be adequately covered there. We'll also use the Apache whenever possible, so it's unlikely I can be intercepted while travelling.

"The office and everything that goes with it will be covered at all times, and will be managed by Sharpe. As a precaution, please let her know of any updates you may have of friends and family off the estate we need to be aware of. Sharpe will deal with all surveillance, communication and logistics. Can you carry your phones with you at all times and make sure they're charged up." And at this he looked around the room, continuing, "You all know who the guilty ones are among you, so get better!" I saw Chloe West and Kay Burton exchange embarrassed looks, the warning not being lost on them.

Cavendish checked what must have been a list of reminders on his clipboard and moved on.

"I want to arrange surveillance cover on the roof. Forster and Peters, can you organise the rota in eight-hour shifts, probably looking at two at a time? You know what to do." He acknowledged Tom Forster's and Oscar Peters's agreement to this, and I looked at the men who, until this moment, I'd thought were the butler and one of the gardeners respectively. It suddenly occurred to me that this was the reasoning behind Cavendish's insistence on the use of surnames. It immediately put the estate on a professional military footing.

I was surprised by his next words.

"Those of you licensed to carry weapons can do so. Make contact with the armoury as necessary, but please ensure you make full use of the firing range to get yourselves up to speed and, more importantly, accurate!"

I didn't even know there was a firing range, or armoury for that matter, but didn't have time to dwell on that now as we were moving on again.

"Now, while the threat has been made against me, I am concerned that Grace and the children are also at risk, but despite my best efforts to get her to leave the estate for a while..." and he fixed Grace with a look as if to check she hadn't changed her mind, to which she responded by smiling and shaking her head slowly. Resigned, he continued, "She won't...so  Sophia and Reuben will be home next week for the holidays, and I don't want them to be affected by this situation any more than can be helped. While they're still at school I'm dispatching Wade and Young to guard them. We'll be taking additional security measures here, but please do nothing that the children could stumble across and get harmed by, and that includes everyone keeping their firearms under wraps – none of us wants Reuben getting hold of anything he shouldn't." At that there were some anxious glances around the room. Reuben was well known for his mischief-making.

"Grayson?"

I looked up quickly, startled as I heard my name, to see Cavendish searching for me. I raised my hand a little self-consciously to draw his attention, my palms becoming clammy as I waited to hear what was to be asked of me.

"Ah, there you are. Now, while we know you're more than capable of looking after yourself..." he paused for the amusement caused by this remark to die down, while I felt myself becoming hot as everyone turned to stare at me. He could only have been referring to the previous altercations I'd been involved in, with Gary and Zoe, and I didn't like the reminder. "...I am concerned you're isolated out there at the stables, and while I'm sure Trent will be there whenever possible..." and at this he and Trent exchanged looks, to more amusement "...I'll need him with me sometimes, so unfortunately he can't be with you all the time. Therefore you'll need to keep particularly vigilant and let us know of any concerns you may have. We'll come and look at the yard and see what we can do to improve security for you. Also, when Grace and the children are there with you this summer, Carlton and Turner are to accompany them. Is that all okay with you?"

I nodded.

"Good...Now, Trent and I will be speaking with all of you over the next few days," Cavendish continued, "to go through what needs to be done for your particular roles, and there will be follow-up briefings. I'm afraid that for the time being all leave is cancelled, and for the safety of everyone your pub nights in the village will have to stop. We can't risk anyone being isolated and picked off. I realise, everyone, that this is going to be challenging. I know you all have jobs to do here as well, but I'm confident that working together we can manage to cover everything as well as protect the estate and everyone on it.

9

"So all of you work on keeping fit and healthy, be vigilant and..." Cavendish paused and looked around the room at all the expectant faces "let us not forget the most important event coming up in the next few weeks, which we also need to prepare for...the wedding of Stanton and Lawson." He grinned at the couple who were standing together by the fireplace. There was a cheer at this reminder, followed by more applause as Cavendish finished speaking, then everyone began to move, the buzz of chatter filling the room once more. Greene leapt up from my side and practically bounced over to Carlton in her excitement.

I stood and looked around me, feeling a bit like a spare part before Trent appeared at my side, slipping his hand into mine, our fingers interlocking. His lips brushed my temple in a gentle kiss as he murmured close to my ear, "Are you okay?"

I nodded, a little unsure as to whether I actually was or not, then said, "It's been quite an eye opener."

"How angry are you with me?"

"I'm not."

Trent raised his eyebrows. "Not too much of a shock?"

"No, though perhaps it hasn't sunk in yet. You've been holding out on me. I hadn't really acknowledged before what you were actually involved in, and I guess I'm feeling a bit out of my depth."

"I didn't want to scare you by telling you any more than you needed to know. I'd hoped it would never come to this."

"Thoughtful as ever." I smiled at him. He tilted his head to one side and gazed at me for a moment.

"So....judging by your reaction, dare I assume you're up for facing the challenges ahead?"

"Always...who doesn't love a challenge?" At the time it seemed so easy to say. As I looked around the room, my gaze drifting from face to face, animated groups, couples talking, Cavendish wrapping his arms around Grace before kissing her, I realised that this was what it had all been about; what we'd been brought together for. To protect this family; this family that inspired loyalty and affection from everyone who surrounded them – their extended family. I knew we were in this together, and in that moment wondered what the future would hold for us.

Half an hour had passed and the office was still full, which was just as well as the door swung open and Forster and Mrs F walked in, each carrying a towering stack of pizza boxes. They were swiftly relieved of their burdens, the boxes placed either on the large coffee table or the desk at the end of the room. The door opened again, this time to Carlton and Ben Hayes carrying a couple of cases of beer. Cheers broke out as the pizzas were handed around and the bottles opened.

I hadn't felt hungry before the food arrived, but once the room started filling with the appetising aroma my mouth watered in anticipation as I reached for a box, and I'd practically finished off an entire pizza before slowing down.

"All this excitement gives a girl an appetite," I mumbled through a mouthful to Trent, who was looking somewhat surprised at the speed with which I'd despatched mine. He hadn't exactly been a slouch either, having already finished. Even so, he was eyeing up my last piece hungrily. I handed it over to him and reached for a couple of beers.

We were ensconced at the end of one of the settees that crowded around the fireplace and large coffee table in this part of the room. I briefly thought back to my interview that had taken place in this same room with only Cavendish and me present. I had been nervous and not expecting to be interviewed by Lord Cavendish at all, and I remembered how I'd wondered then what sort of occasion would have required the need for there to be so much seating. Now here we were. I could never have imagined it.

An hour or so passed. No big plans were being made now. This was not the time for that. This was the time for camaraderie; for forming friendships, strengthening bonds.

I'd made some good friends here already, but now there was the chance to chat to others I didn't know so much about. My daily life at the stables didn't bring me into regular contact with everyone else on the estate, and while I was not an outgoing person I felt, with what was in store for us, it was going to become important that I knew who was around me, and that they, in turn, knew more about me – or at least as much as I was willing for them to know – so I needed to make the effort.

I even managed to introduce myself to the elusive Sharpe. We shook hands firmly. She was no less intimidating up close than she'd been from across the room. I was definitely a little ragged around the edges beside her coiffed perfection. Perfect nails; perfect make up; not a hair out of place. Like I'd thought, intimidating. I also got the distinct impression I was being inspected as we talked. It wasn't that she wasn't friendly exactly, but there was something that was a little off, a little uptight.

Trent came over while I was talking to her, to join in our conversation, I'd assumed, but pretty soon he reminded me of the time and suggested I needed to get back to see to the yard. I made my excuses to Sharpe and turned to leave, though as we went to the other end of the room it suddenly occurred to me that he wasn't coming with me.

"Cavendish needs you here tonight, doesn't he?"

"Actually, no. Tonight I'm all yours, so we need to make the most of it." He smiled at me. "I have a couple of things to sort out here first though, but if you go now I should be back by the time you've finished the yard." Not

12

wanting to waste a second of our time together, I said a quick group goodbye to everyone and left to return to the stables.

I let Susie out first, and, pleased to see me as always, she accompanied me while I checked on the horses and topped up the water for each stable. All was calm in the yard, and after the summer winds that had brought the day's showers and rustled through the surrounding trees, all was now still. A promise of better weather to come, perhaps. I'd just got back to the cottage when Trent arrived.

I turned to him in the kitchen, sliding my arms around him under the unfamiliar lightweight jacket he was wearing casually with his jeans and tee shirt. Stopping abruptly, he tensed as I brushed against the object under his left arm. I pulled back, my arms falling to my sides as I glanced up at him warily, catching his uneasiness as he looked away. I reached out and gingerly opened the left side of his jacket. Now I could see the butt of the gun as it nestled in its holster. I swallowed, uncertain what to say. I should have realised, of course.

"Well this is new...and weird," I muttered almost to myself as my eyes flicked back up to his face. "I should've been expecting this, I guess. Should've known you'd be licensed to carry a gun."

"I know it's going to be difficult for you...having this here...after.." and he hesitated, not wanting to finish, not wanting to bring up what we were both thinking, remembering. Remembering the last time there'd been a gun in this house, the only time I'd ever touched one before and the tragedy that had befallen the person – Zoe, Trent's ex-wife – who had brought it here. A tragedy that had been caused by my hand and that was still fresh, and painful, in both our minds.

"It is what it is, Trent," I said. "Let's not waste time on things we can't change." I reached one hand up to his face,

13

my fingers in his hair as I brought his lips to mine and felt his breath catch as he took me in his arms.

## Chapter 2

By the morning I didn't feel so positive. The previous
night I'd been buoyed by the camaraderie of being among
the others, when it had seemed that anything was possible.
Now...I wanted to say "In the cold light of day", but that
wouldn't have been right. This day had dawned bright,
sunny and was going to be hot. I, however, felt a chill. My
concerns were growing because I perceived that the
chance of a successful outcome for the situation that we
were all facing was unlikely. As I fed the horses, the more
I thought about it, the more out of sorts I became. I didn't
come from a military background like everyone else here;
I hadn't had the training that would prepare me for this,
either mentally or physically. How could we possibly
defend this place, this family? By the time I got back to the
cottage to join Trent for breakfast a deep unease had
settled over me. I had a million questions I wanted to
bombard him with: about the work he'd been doing, about
everyone on the estate, why they were there and the roles
each was going to play in the situation evolving around us.
However I knew I'd have to rein back as he was weary
after his latest trip which, while he'd made light of it, had
still left him with a black eye and bruised ribs. Both would
take some getting over, and I didn't want him closing up
on me. So as we sat eating toast and drinking tea I pushed
aside my real concerns and started with my newest
acquaintance.

"It was good to finally put a face to a name when I met
Sharpe last night."

"Yes, I'd forgotten you hadn't met her before, sorry. I
should have made the effort to get you to come to the

office at some point to introduce you, but it slipped my mind."

"It's not a problem...but, can I ask, is she always that intense?"

He frowned. "What do you mean by intense?"

"It wasn't as if she wasn't perfectly friendly, more that I felt as if I was under some sort of scrutiny."

"Ah." He hesitated, looking away before grinning at me a little sheepishly. "If memory serves me correctly she makes a particularly fine beef in red wine." I looked at him blankly. He raised his eyebrows at me as if nudging my thought processes.

"Oh..." I remembered Trent telling me how attempts had been made by some on the estate to seduce him in the past, using the lure of food. "No wonder she was studying me so closely, she must have wondered what on earth you could possibly see in someone so untidily turned out."

"Yes, she is a little fastidious. You can imagine what she's like running an office, can't you? However, her nature makes her perfect for us. She's our organisational hub, and everything runs like clockwork under her diligent eye."

"So how is office work going to be of use in this situation then?" I questioned, baffled.

"Her day-to-day job here is running the estate office, but in this situation she'll be incorporating her more extensive skills which cover surveillance, communication and logistics.

She manages all the systems on the estate, such as the one controlling the main gates which we're going to have a look at today as we'll have to bring in something a little more secure.

"The gate system will link in and enhance the rest of our surveillance on the estate. Some is already in place and only needs to be turned on, and some is still to be looked at. The office is set up as a monitoring centre for the surveillance system, which Sharpe also manages together with the logistics for the estate. Any services or equipment that are needed she gets them, working closely with Grace, Mrs F and Mrs Bray."

"That seems like a lot for one person to deal with," I commented, thinking I'd find that amount of organisation overwhelming.

"That's what makes her indispensible: her capacity and apparent enjoyment for the work. Obviously she'll bring in others as and when needed on this, particularly for monitoring the surveillance screens."

"And she lives off the estate?"

"Yes, she's been living with a guy called Mark in the village for a couple of years now. You'll meet him at the wedding I should think. Anyway..." he glanced at his watch "I'd better get off to the Manor. Cavendish and I are going to make a start this morning by going round the perimeter of the estate to see if there is anything we can do to improve security. It's a bit difficult though because the only thing that will really make a difference is to fix barbed wire along the top of the wall. If we did that it would not only draw unwanted attention to us but would cause great consternation to those in the surrounding villages who would start wondering what we were running here. Our cover of this only being a productive agricultural estate would be blown."

He paused, looking a bit uncomfortable. "Before I get off though one thing I wanted to ask...well, we wanted to ask..." He hesitated, before continuing, "We were wondering if you wanted to have some firearms training?"

My immediate reaction was a definite no, and I shook my head vigorously. There was no way I wanted to get involved with that. I was happy never to touch a gun again.

Trent held his hands up, pacifying me. "It's all right, Em, I thought as much...if you change your mind though let us know, okay?"

17

"Okay," I mumbled, hating the whole idea.

He was quiet as he finished his tea, then asked, "Do you have any plans for the day?"

In that moment my decision was made. "Yes, actually I've decided that I'm going to visit Eva. I suddenly feel the need." I was surprised by the look of concern that flickered across his face as I said this.

"Oh, I didn't realise you were thinking of doing that." He hesitated pensively. "I'd like to come with you..." I could see he was torn between what he had to do today, things I knew he couldn't put off, and what he wanted to do, with me.

"It's fine, Trent, I appreciate the thought but I'm not expecting you to drop everything and come with me."

"It's not that..." He looked uneasy. "Couldn't you leave it until next week? We're due to go there anyway for Zoe's interment."

I didn't need reminding. "I feel the need to go now. Who knows when things could kick off here and I may not get another chance. Everything might be cancelled next week for all we know. I'll be fine...okay?"

"Okay...keep in touch, will you?" He still looked, and sounded, a little disgruntled.

"Of course." I tried to reassure him. Why was he so concerned? As he went to get ready to leave I pondered on this. Maybe it was because of the situation the estate was currently facing; maybe he didn't want me wandering about on my own...maybe.

Mondays were usually the horses' day off from exercise, so once Trent had left I went to turn them out, mucked out the stables and prepared everything for the evening. I returned to the cottage, changed into some clean clothes and made sure Susie would be staying in by locking the cat flap. I drove off in the pickup, turned left out of the yard, away from the Manor, and, passing in front of the cottage, headed for the main gate. I would normally have taken my own car on this trip, but since that had been burnt out by Zoe I had no choice. I knew Cavendish wouldn't mind, but still didn't like taking advantage of his good nature.

As I passed through the main gate I kept a look out for Trent and the others, half expecting that they would be there reviewing security, but there was no sign of anyone.

I drove to Crowbridge, pleased to have some time away to think through all that was happening. The revelations made the night before of what Cavendish and Trent were involved in and the consequences their actions were now going to bring to us all certainly gave me plenty to occupy my mind on the journey.

I entered the village of Crowbridge, not allowing myself to dwell on the life I'd once had there, and turned up towards the church. Parking beside another car and picking up the small bunch of flowers I'd quickly gathered from my garden before leaving, I set off for the churchyard.

As soon as I walked through the oaken gate at the entrance I saw him. I paused for a moment, deliberating, wondering if I should turn back, leave him to his privacy. I watched him as he stood, head bowed, hands thrust into his jeans pockets, his arms tanned, his golden hair accentuated in the sunlight. This man whom I'd once loved so much, but who had betrayed me. Finally I decided that this moment was going to come one day, and it was probably best to get it over with.

Walking towards him I didn't think he'd hear me coming, so I cleared my throat as I approached, not wanting to make him jump. He spun round, his face briefly lighting up with the surprise of seeing me.

"Hi, Em!" His initial enthusiasm disappeared almost immediately, replaced by a wariness I didn't understand as he looked beyond me, checking out the entrance, scanning the rest of the churchyard.

"Alex," I replied slowly as I looked round to where he was looking, trying to see whatever it was he was searching for. "Are you okay?"

"Fine, yeah, how are you? What've you been up to?" He was edgy and still distracted by our surroundings for some reason.

"I'm fine too." I left it at that, thinking it was probably best not to mention that I'd been shot and stabbed since the last time I'd seen him. I'd also killed someone – mustn't forget that.

"Alex.." I could hear the question start even as I spoke his name, "what's going on?"

He drew his attention back to me. "Are you here on your own or...or is Trent here somewhere?" I could hear an anxious note in his voice.

"I'm here on my own," I confirmed, puzzled, then even more so as he visibly relaxed.

"Oh, okay...come and sit down then." And he lifted his hand towards me, not touching but guiding me to the bench he indicated with his other hand. I sat, mystified as to the reason for his behaviour. He joined me, and we were silent for a moment in quiet contemplation of our daughter's grave directly in front of us. I turned to him.

"What's going on, Alex? Why are you concerned if Trent's with me or not?" I could feel my spirits dropping with the disappointment that crept over me, a feeling that I already knew the answers to the questions I was raising but I didn't want to voice them. He tried to appear as if nothing was wrong, but after our years together I knew he was hiding something and pressed him for an answer, unsurprised when it came.

"He doesn't want me to see you, to have anything to do with you in fact. He made that very clear." He watched me steadily. I looked away, deep in thought. When Alex had come to Melton a few weeks back and met Trent in the pub there'd been obvious tension between them, but nothing of this nature had been specifically said and I couldn't think why Alex would say it now. Suddenly it came to me and I looked back up at him sharply.

"He's been to see you." Alex gave a small sigh of relief that I'd come to this realisation.

"He's been to see me," he repeated, nodding. "He's a dangerous man, Em." He shifted uncomfortably and in this short phrase I could see the difference between them: Alex's easygoing lightness set against the darkness of Trent. Alex continued, "I thought perhaps you'd sent him...which is what hurt more. But I can see now by your reaction, by the fact that your eyebrows have just shot up your forehead, that you didn't." He smiled at my expression of astonishment. I was surprised he would have thought that of me.

"I fight my own battles, Alex, you know that...and now it looks as if I shall have another one to face when I get home," I muttered, as if to myself.

"I don't envy him that...*if* you're sure you can handle him." He hesitated. "I don't like you being with him, Em."

My immediate thought was that it was no longer his concern, but I realised my reaction had been tempered. A short while ago I would have found his words irritating; now for some reason I found them comforting, knowing he still cared.

"What did he do to you?" I questioned, concerned. He looked uncomfortable and shrugged.

"Nothing actually...nothing physical, anyway...he didn't have to...it was implied. He made his intentions perfectly clear." And I knew that Trent would have done; he had that way about him, and knowing my feeling of disappointment hadn't been misplaced made me angry. Angry that he had done this to Alex, angry because I'd told him Alex was no threat and angry that he couldn't leave it alone. But my anger would have to wait for the moment as I felt the need to reassure Alex.

"I'm sorry if you felt threatened by him in any way but you don't need to worry, Alex. I'll make sure he doesn't come near you again, and he would never do anything to me, I can promise you that. He's...a little possessive, that's all, and he sees you as a threat."

Alex gave me a small smile, and said wistfully, "I wish I was...then it would be worth taking the beating he was offering to hand out." Despite his bravado and the fact that he was not exactly backwards in the macho stakes himself, I knew he would be no match for Trent. He probably knew that as well.

"Those days have gone...I told you."

"I know," his resignation clear in his tone and he looked away

I moved off the bench then and knelt on the ground. Dampness from the previous day's rain seeped into my jeans as I started to tidy up the grave.

Alex and I had lost Eva through a sudden illness when she was six. I'd been devastated by her loss, and now, five years later, I'd only just started dealing with it. Alex had abandoned me to have an affair with my then best friend as our marriage crumbled under the strain of our grief and I'd found myself alone, having no family alive to support me. Crushed beneath an unbearable load of depression and guilt, it had been Trent who had helped me. Despite being together only a short while it had been he who'd encouraged me to open up and talk about Eva with him, and this had brought back happier memories, things I could share, and I now had a much healthier perspective on my previous life. I knew Cavendish and Grace were the only other people on the estate who knew about Eva. I hadn't been able to bring myself to tell anyone else. It was one of the reasons why I'd gone to the estate in the first place: to start again where no one knew my past; where no one took pity on me.

I replaced the dead flowers at the base of the headstone with the flowers I'd brought. When I'd finished I sat back on the bench. Alex hadn't uttered a word while I'd done this, and we continued to sit quietly until suddenly it came to me. As I sat surrounded by all that I'd lost I knew the reason for the disquiet hanging over me. Loss. Or, more precisely, fear of loss. I knew I couldn't face losing anyone else from my life, and the impending threat against Cavendish and, by association, all on the estate, a threat approaching as surely as the rolling clouds of a storm, seemed certain to bring misery with it.

Rolling my shoulders to release the tension that had built up in them, I felt a certain level of relief as soon as I'd reached this conclusion. I imagined it was the sort of relief experienced by a patient when a diagnosis was made: the prognosis might still be terrible, but at least you knew what you were dealing with. I assumed that knowing what the problem was surely meant a solution could be found. I knew I could never revisit the dark months of grieving I'd gone through after Eva had died. It had been a truly terrible time and, I reasoned, somehow I needed to protect myself against the chance of it ever happening again.

At this distance it felt that the simplest, the easiest, thing to do would be to remove myself from the situation evolving on the estate. Actually, it wouldn't be the easiest thing to do at all, but if I left what I didn't know wouldn't hurt me, and once my thoughts started in this direction I couldn't think beyond that. Could I walk away? Or was I being naive? Was it because I was at this distance that it seemed like the best option to take? The questions jumbled together in my mind and I couldn't resolve them now. Knowing what the problem was had made me feel calmer, but I had to deal with other matters first and, pushing my concerns to the back of my mind, I turned my attention back to Alex.

"I'm glad you still come to see her, Alex. I wasn't sure if you did or not."

"Of course I do, I'm just not that good at bringing flowers." He cleared his throat before asking quietly, "Do you ever think about how things might have been for us now, Em, if Eva hadn't died...if I hadn't messed up?"

"I used to...all the time...but not any more." I shook my head slowly. "It made me so miserable constantly thinking about how she would have changed, imagining our lives as they would have been if we'd still been together, imagining doing all the things we'd said we would do with her. It was exhausting and I couldn't afford to expend any more energy on it. Eventually I faced up to the fact that her life had ended and nothing could change what had happened." I looked over at him and knew from his expression he'd been in the same place. He nodded, understanding where my mind was at, then stood silently, turning to go before he looked back at me, meeting my eyes as I read the sadness in his.

"Look after yourself, Em...and if you ever need me, just call. I'll always be here for you." Without waiting for a response, he walked away.

I watched him leave, and as he went I realised for the first time that I felt genuine concern for him. The bitterness and animosity I'd carried that had eaten away at me like a cancer as it poisoned every thought and feeling I'd had towards him over such a long time had at last gone.

I turned back to Eva, and for as long as I could I allowed my thoughts and feelings to be swamped by her as I told her about my life at Melton. I updated her with tales of the horses, Susie, the simple things. In due course, however, my thoughts returned to the problems I was facing back at the estate. I had two issues to deal with: Trent's possessiveness and my fear. I was ashamed of the fear. Everyone else on the estate was brave, fearless – I'd seen it in their reactions at the meeting last night. I'd been carried along on the wave of camaraderie, but I was a fraud pretending to be something I wasn't. I hated to admit that to myself, let alone someone else, and I didn't know what to do, not for certain. I feared what staying on the estate would bring, and I knew it wouldn't be easy to leave. Just the thought of it, of what it would do to Trent, of how it'd make me feel, made me nauseous, but sitting here in the peaceful sunshine it seemed the best solution, at least for me. Getting up to leave the churchyard, I passed back through the gate and wondered how I was going to approach this with Trent. Then, thinking back to his overzealous possessiveness, the first prickles of anger started to make their presence felt and I knew my course of action.

# Chapter 3

My thoughts as I drove back were confused, flipping to and fro on whether to stay or not, weighing up the pros and cons of the choices before me. By the time I arrived at the main gate, narrowly missing a dark blue car that was pulling away, its tinted windows obscuring its occupants, I was none the wiser on the route I would take, but my anger, caused by Trent's possessiveness, had intensified to a level that I knew I could use. I wasn't so selfish as to interrupt his work at this time, but deciding I needed to tackle him about that issue sooner rather than later I thought I'd see if he was available. As soon as I passed through the main gate I stopped and, facing the road that led straight to the Manor, checked my phone which I'd put on silent. There were several unread messages and missed calls from him. I sent a text asking where he was. He called immediately in response, sounding grumpy.

"About time – I've been trying to contact you. I asked you to stay in touch."

I wasn't about to react to that. "Where are you?"

"I'm in the woodland, the other side of the Manor."

"Are you busy?"

"I'm about to finish...we're cutting back some trees for sight lines. Are you..."

I cut him off, then turned away from the route to the stables and drove along the other lane until I saw his truck parked, partly hidden, among the trees. The red pickup was there too, but from the road I couldn't see who else was around. I pulled over, got out and headed towards where I could now see a small group of them working. They'd removed some branches from nearby trees and were busy cutting them up. There was a small bonfire going which, from the amount of smoke it produced, was disposing of the greenery.

Trent looked up, silent, when he saw me approaching, and I felt him study me, his eyes narrowing as he frowned, trying to gauge my mood which he must have guessed wasn't good. The sleeves of his red checked shirt were rolled up over his strong forearms, his jaw clenched as he watched me with his unwavering blue-eyed stare, his dark and unruly hair made me want to be running my fingers through it – but I firmly banished that thought from my head.

I walked towards him purposefully, not losing eye contact, not wanting to say anything in front of the others. Fortunately they were occupied; Carlton wielding a chainsaw, Hayes stacking logs into the back of the pickup and Josh Turner manning the bonfire. I walked straight past Trent and carried on going, deeper into the woods. For a while I didn't think he'd followed and started to wonder what my next move should be, but then I heard the snap of a twig.

"Where are we going?" he asked.

"Out of earshot." He stayed behind me, presumably considering why that would be needed. When I thought we'd gone far enough I stopped, pausing for a long moment, and then, taking a deep breath, turned back towards him. He'd stopped at the same time as me and there were now ten feet or so between us. I wanted, very much, to keep my anger in check.

"Is there anything that you think you should tell me?" My voice was quiet, calm. He looked puzzled as he cautiously answered.

"I don't think so. What's the matter, Em? You're worrying me."

I held his eyes. "Trent...I want you to think very carefully about what you say next." I paused. "Think about where I've been today, and think again about whether there is anything you should tell me."

I watched him closely, waiting for the reaction that I knew would come. I saw the realisation hit along with a flash of anger across his face. He exhaled loudly as he exclaimed, "You met with him!"

Don't rise to the accusation, I told myself firmly.

"I didn't meet with him...we bumped into each other."

"How very convenient," he retorted.

"We share the common ground of our daughter's grave, Trent."

At this he did at least have the grace to look abashed. I gave him some time before I continued, "What did you do to him?"

"Nothing. Why? What did he tell you I did? Come running to you with his tales of woe, did he? And why would you be upset about me doing anything to him anyway?"

"He described you as dangerous."

"You already knew that."

"How dangerous, Trent?"

"You know I'm capable of killing with my bare hands – how dangerous do you want me to be?"

I did know that, it being the reason he was no longer in the RAF, but I had wondered on the drive back if there was something else; something Alex had seen in him that I hadn't, but as I didn't think I was going to get him to elaborate on this now I moved on.

"I'd already dealt with him, Trent, there was no need for you to do anything. I told you that, but you wouldn't listen to me, wouldn't leave it alone. Now he's concerned that I'm with a 'dangerous' man, and he's not at all happy about that."

"I couldn't care less whether he's happy or not."

"Well I could...I don't wish him any harm, Trent. I just want him to go and get on with his own life."

"I've seen what he did to you, Em. I've seen how much he hurt you. And as you did not make it clear, at least not clear enough for me, what I was to you, I wanted to make sure that he understood, that we were on the same page and that he was going to keep away from you."

"What you are to me can change, Trent," I snapped, instantly regretting those ill-chosen words as I saw the hurt on his face. By his reaction I knew that if I decided to go it was going to be harder to put into practice than I'd first thought.

He gathered himself for a moment before continuing in a more conciliatory tone, "I don't understand how you can feel so equable towards him."

"I've given him a hard time for far too long. Losing Eva...what we went through together was more terrible than you can possibly imagine, and we failed to come out of it complete. I've spent a lot of time and far too much energy ruminating on what he did to me...and now I'm here..." and I paused, hesitating over my next words.

He filled them in. "...And with you...is that what you were about to say?"

"Yes," I replied, my throat tightening, "and I need to let it go." I paused as I took a breath and steadied myself. "I'm more concerned about your possessiveness, the fact that you feel you have to involve yourself in a situation that has nothing to do with you. You've brought yourself to his attention in a way that wasn't necessary, and you shouldn't have done that. I don't want there to be ongoing trouble between you."

"You may think he's tough, but he's no threat to me."

"This is exactly what I'm talking about – why do you feel so aggressively towards him?"

"I feel the way I do because of what he did to you, and I don't understand why you don't feel like that."

I thought carefully before answering, hoping to get my point across. "I don't feel that way any more, Trent, because he was the man I once loved so much that I chose him to have a child with. I don't love him any more, but neither do I hate him in the way I did. Time has healed the heartache he caused me."

"You think it's time that's 'healed' you, do you? You don't think it's possible that it's me that's helped, the way we feel for each other that's enabled you to move on?"

I hadn't thought of it like that, and I pondered on this, though was unable to address it, knowing it would weaken my argument for leaving, if I ever got to that, so I went on as if it hadn't been raised.

"I just want him to go his own way and have a chance to be happy again."

Trent was silent, staring at me. Then his voice rose accusingly. "Has he wormed his way back into your affections? Is that it? Tried to get into your good books by telling you about me threatening him?"

Unbelievable. I exhaled loudly in exasperation. I was getting nowhere and was struggling not to yell at him. Somehow I managed to respond and still sound fairly reasonable.

"Of course he hasn't...I only realised today that I don't have all those negative feelings towards him any more – whatever the reason." Frustrated at my apparent inability to get through to him I turned away to walk back to my pickup. I felt tears welling, ridiculously saddened by the argument I'd instigated but now didn't have the energy to prolong or see through to the bitter end I'd planned. One issue at a time, I thought. He caught up with me, placing a hand on my upper arm as if to stop me, but I shook it off.

"Em, don't walk away. I'll come back with you..."

"Don't," I said, without stopping or looking at him, "and don't come round this evening. I need some time...and I suggest you take that time as well."

"Em, I've only got this evening to be with you. I'm then with Cavendish overnight."

I climbed into the pickup.

"Then maybe I'll see you tomorrow," and I drove off.

Back at the stables, I let Susie out before making a fuss of her while I had a cup of tea. She jumped up on to my lap as I sat at the kitchen table, and every time I stopped caressing her scruffy little ears, her favourite stroking spot, she nudged her head up under my hand to encourage me to go on. I felt twitchy, doubts gnawing at my stomach; I didn't like being at odds with Trent. As always, Susie eased me. She was the one constant in my life, and had been endlessly patient and tolerant of me when I must have been a difficult person to be around. Susie held my darkest thoughts and fears without reproach, and I was pleased I'd been able to repay her faithfulness by bringing her here where it was safe for her to wander around and have so much freedom. Though that could now be changing, I thought sadly.

It was time to get the horses in, so we both walked out to the paddock. Monty had already had enough and was waiting by the gate, so I brought him in first, gave him a quick brush over and put him in his stable. I went back to get each of the others in, and when I'd finished I headed back to the cottage and went straight to the fridge. Taking out a bottle of white wine, I was reaching for a glass when I saw Greene crossing the yard. I made it two glasses, and intercepted her as she came up the garden path.

"Join me?" I asked, lifting the glasses so she could see what I was referring to.

"Like that, is it?" Greene took a seat at the garden table and slid her sunglasses up so they sat on top of her head. I poured out the wine and we sat for a few minutes in silence, enjoying our peaceful surroundings on this warm summer evening. Greene was that sort of friend. I knew that, like me, she'd come here for a new start, also having come out of a long-term relationship, and although we'd agreed not to dwell on our pasts, I felt her to be a kindred spirit. She took a large sip then, putting her glass down, looked over at me and I wondered what was coming.

"Have you two had a row?"

"Yes...well, sort of...how do you know?"

"Carlton thought as much."

"Did he hear us then?" Should've gone further into the woods, I thought.

"No, he guessed. He said Trent was off all day, and then you arrived looking frosty and walked off with him. When Trent returned he was pretty pissed off. Do you want to talk about it?"

I took a large gulp of my wine. "It's a long story."

"Don't tell me if you'd rather not."

"No...I think it's about time I did." I took a deep breath and told her everything, even about Eva. I hadn't been able to bring myself to speak of this most private part of my life before, but we were now good friends. I trusted her, and I knew she'd keep it between herself and Carlton.

When I'd finished she didn't speak for a few moments, but reached out and placed her hand over mine, squeezing it gently.

"Bloody hell, Grayson, I wasn't expecting that. Never having had a child I can't imagine everything you've been through...though I always knew there was something. I could sense it, but never realised quite how terrible it would be..." She shook her head, then swallowed the last of her wine. She didn't dwell on the past as I knew she wouldn't and moved on. "So...what're you going to do about Trent now?"

I didn't want to reveal the depth of my fears to her, so I decided not to fill her in on my possible plan to leave. I didn't want someone else's opinion muddying the waters of my indecision.

"I told him not to come round tonight. We both need time to cool off and think this through. But he needs to know that he has to tone down the possessiveness a notch or two. I can't have him going off after people, threatening them."

"No, that is a bit extreme," Greene agreed as I topped up our glasses. She went on carefully, "Though I think it's only his way of showing you he cares."

"Don't you start defending or making excuses for him...or I shall start regretting my decision to banish him for the evening," I said, smiling. She took the cue not to press for him any further, and we moved on to less challenging topics of conversation. As we talked, she made me laugh with some tale or other about her and Carlton, and I realised how much I envied their easygoing relationship. I was pleased they were getting on so well. There had been a time when Carlton and I had nearly had a moment; a moment that had been thwarted by Trent – another example of his possessiveness. But I was pleased now that Carlton and I were only friends; he and Greene were much better suited to each other.

Greene left a little while later, by which time we were both feeling rather mellow, and I went in to do my exercises. I'd been given these by the physiotherapist to do while recovering from being shot, and I tried to do them twice a day. My shoulder was healing well, and although the scar still looked pink and fresh, the exercises were helping to improve the flexibility and build up my strength. The physiotherapist had also worked with me in sessions at the gym, and I'd recently started going back to do my usual, though appropriately modified, workout. Before the shooting I'd been fit and I didn't want my fitness levels to drop, so it was good to be back in my routine. I'd even started practising my kickboxing again, and fitted in some punches and kicks on the punch bag at the end of each session. I was going to give it a miss this evening, though, obviously not wanting to bump into Trent.

I showered when I'd finished, then, as nothing else in the fridge appealed, I munched some crackers and cheese by way of supper before turning my attention to packing. I thought I'd take some sort of decisive action. As Cavendish had paid for my riding clothes I'd leave them behind. Otherwise I didn't have much more than I'd had when I arrived here little more than a year ago. One case and a couple of boxes, including the one filled with Eva's things. As I packed I pondered on how I was going to go about this, but the more I thought the more muddled I became. I decided I'd go and see Cavendish the next day and explain. Explain what? That I was running; leaving them in the lurch; leaving them with even more to do. I felt a surge of shame at what I was planning. They'd been so good to me and I would be letting them down. I was being selfish, but what else could I do? I wasn't brave and strong like everyone else here, and I was afraid I was going to end up right back where I had been and I couldn't cope with that. I sat on the edge of my bed, my head in my hands and my mind in turmoil, not knowing what to do.

Shortly after ten I went out to check on the horses, topped up their water buckets, then, decided on an early night, hoping sleep would resolve my problems, but spent the next couple of hours tossing and turning in a fruitless quest for it. At around midnight, irritated by my inability to doze off, I got up and padded back downstairs, thinking I might watch a film. I went to the sink to get some water first, and as I did I glanced out of the window and was surprised to see Trent's truck parked just beyond my garden fence. I looked down at Susie, who had come to greet my unusual nocturnal wanderings.

"I think I preferred it when you didn't like him. At least then I'd get some warning of his approach." She stared at me for a moment before returning to her bed, no doubt thinking there was nothing she could do for me now. I'd asked him not to come round, yet here he was, not listening, again. I unlocked the back door and walked down the path as he got out of the truck. He stood at the end of the path, not taking another step, as if this boundary marked the line he should not cross. I stopped the other side of the invisible divide and watched him silently.

"I'm sorry."

"What are you sorry for, Trent?"

"Clearly you don't find my possessiveness one of my more endearing qualities, so I'm sorry for going to see Alex...and I shall try harder not to behave like that again."

"Do you trust me?"

"Yes, but I don't trust him, I'm afraid, and it's in my nature to be possessive of you. I don't want to lose you...to someone else."

"You won't lose me to someone else, but you will lose me if you do this again because I don't want to live like that." He nodded in what I hoped was agreement and understanding, then silently he continued to study me.

"I think there is something else, Em."

"I don't know what you mean," I replied, sounding defiant, but I did know, and I knew he could see straight through me.

"I think you're using this argument to distract me from the real problem." His words were measured, his tone even, and I hated the fact he was so controlled.

Unable to tell him, I thought I'd continue with the distraction. "How come you're here anyway? I thought you were on Cavendish duty tonight."

"I was, but Carlton turned up and offered to relieve me."

I hesitated, thoughtful. "We have good friends."

He nodded in agreement as he repeated, "We have good friends."

"So you thought you'd come and sit outside my cottage, even though I told you I didn't want to see you...were you planning on sitting there all night?"

"If need be. I've told you before, I don't like to be away from you when I don't have to be." He looked at me a little sheepishly. "I suppose I hoped you wouldn't be able to sleep and would come and take pity on me." And he gave me a small smile while slowly lifting his hand towards me. I didn't like the fact that he appeared to know me so well, but he was right, I couldn't settle when there was animosity between us. I didn't make a move towards taking his hand though, and as I watched him he tilted his head thoughtfully. I felt him assessing me.

"I know there's something else, Emma, what is it?"

My mouth was suddenly dry. I swallowed. "I'm not sure I'm going to be staying here, Trent."

That shook his confident demeanour. He looked dumbfounded, and it was some time before he found his voice. "For Christ's sake, Emma, why do you want to leave? Are you still having second thoughts about us? I've told you I'll change, but you need to give me a chance." He shook his head in disbelief and my heart lurched. How could I do this to him? He reached for me, but I moved away before he made contact, knowing if he did I wouldn't be able to go on.

He stared at me. "Tell me."

I looked down nervously, gathering my thoughts, trying to hold fast to my resolution. "It's self-preservation." I hated having to admit this to myself, let alone out loud, feeling my face colour as I said feebly, "I'm afraid."

Astonishingly, he looked relieved.

"Of course you are. With what we're facing I'd be worried about you if you weren't. But that's what we're all here for, Em. That's why we've put this together so that we work together, support each other in doing what needs to be done. You're out of the way at the stables, you're going to be fine." He was trying to reassure me but I shook my head, my eyes downcast, not wanting to meet his. My fingers picked at a rough piece of nail.

"That's not what I'm afraid of, Trent. Well...obviously, that's part of it, but that's not what's behind me leaving." I paused for a moment before deciding to come right out and say it. "I can't face the possibility of losing anyone else...of losing you."

"But I'm not going to be going anywhere."

"That may not be your decision to make."

He was silent for a moment as he sorted through my words.

"So you're thinking it would be better to go now and definitely lose me rather than stay here with a vague possibility of losing me in the future?" He was clearly baffled by my reasoning, and I had to admit it didn't make a great deal of sense when put that way. I could suggest that we left together, but knew that would be a non-starter of an idea. He would never leave, and I knew I'd never put him in the position of having to decide.

Trent exhaled, running his fingers through his hair in exasperation. "Look, Emma, I'm sorry I've put you in this situation, but stay, please. *If* something were to happen to me, you would be surrounded here by people who love and care for you. It's important to me to know that you're looked after and that you wouldn't ever be alone again." He was trying to placate me. "You know we don't do well when we're apart. We've been there before – think back, Em, think about how you felt then, how bad it was and how bad it would be now if you left." And I remembered with brutal clarity the time we'd spent apart after our row and before Zoe had attacked me; how heartbreaking it was; how miserable I'd been.

He continued, his voice soft, "Do you really think that you can walk away from this?" He brought his hand up and moved it slowly back and forth between our bodies, indicating to whatever it was that breathed in the space between us, the longing that pulled us together, making us whole. I was lost. In that moment I knew my idea to leave had been a ludicrous one. I knew that it would hurt as much as having a limb ripped from me.

Sensing me wavering, he once again lifted his hand up from his side and stretched towards me in supplication. I reached my hand forward, feeling the familiar spark as I touched his fingers, gliding my hand softly over his, letting it continue up his arm. His skin felt cool and dry against mine. Closing the distance between us, he brought his mouth to my neck, kissing it tenderly, his lips caressing slowly upward, along the line of my jaw, my cheek. Questioning and hesitant he found my lips and I melted under him as he breathed, "Please tell me we can make up now?"

"Mmmm" was the only response I could manage, and at this encouragement he swept me up into his arms and carried me back into the cottage.

I thought we were going to bed but Trent thought otherwise carrying me through to the sitting room before putting me down. His kisses, as he held me tight up against him, were filled with an urgency that made me hot and needy and within moments we were stripped and going at it on the settee. He arched over me, gazing down, his eyes never leaving mine as he thrust into me, his muscles taut and straining for release as he held on and I felt exposed as he watched me unravelling beneath him and wondered how I thought for one moment I could have left him.

We did most of our making up on the settee before finally ending up in bed where I fell into a deep and restful sleep, and woke to find him still wrapped around me in the morning.

# Chapter 4

Cavendish arrived shortly after breakfast the next morning to discuss the security at the stables. After my encounter with Zoe a panic button had been put in my bedroom, in addition to the one in the kitchen, so not much more could be done to the cottage. Trent and Cavendish therefore concentrated on the yard while I tacked up Regan and got Benjy ready to lead out.

Before I set off, they outlined their plans to install a couple of cameras in the trees on the perimeters of the yard. These would cover the back of the cottage as well as the stables, and capture anyone wandering around. I didn't like the thought of someone watching me, even if it was for my safety and the safety of others, but knew I was going to have to put up with it. Once they were satisfied they'd covered everything they left, and I followed them out of the yard on my first ride of the day.

I felt better after my previous day's wobble, if a little foolish. I'd been more affected by the announcements made at the meeting than I cared to admit, and going to see Eva, and Alex, had just pushed me over the edge into making some stupid decisions. It wasn't like me to run away, and I was annoyed with myself for being so weak. Fortunately Trent hadn't made any further mention of it, and if he'd noticed the packed case he didn't comment on it. Now, though, I was back, and while I was still afraid, I was also determined to face whatever life was about to throw at me. Whatever that was, I knew I'd come through worse already.

It felt good to be back to my normal routine and I worked through the day, finishing with a trip to the gym followed by a much-needed shower. Trent arrived soon after, and we ate dinner together before he had to leave to take up his duty with Cavendish.

The next few days saw an increased amount of activity on the estate. Cameras were installed, not only around the stables but also at the farmyard, and a couple were added to the Manor in addition to those already installed there. The main gate had a new entry system which meant our magic buttons no longer worked. There was now a camera that scanned each driver, and a password had to be given before entry was granted. The password was specific to each estate worker, and we all had to go to the Manor and set up our password entry with Sharpe. This involved giving her one password for everyday use. A second password was then set up which was to be used if you were under duress when giving it. Sharpe made it all seem very normal; to me, it felt anything but.

I had to go to the vet to pick up some supplies one day and decided to go via the farmyard rather than face the kerfuffle of getting out of the main gate, only to find that leaving that way was now equally demanding. The five-barred gates were closed and locked, and sheets of metal had been attached to them, making them some ten feet high and solid. Adam Porter, the farm manager, came out to unlock them and let me out. He said he'd be around to let me in on my return, but I didn't want to put him out so told him I'd return by the main gate.

I also received a phone call from the police informing me that no charges were going to be made against me over Zoe's death. It was what we'd expected, but was still a relief to have confirmed. However, this good news was overshadowed by the fact that I had to attend the inquest into her death which was to resume at the end of the week. To be fair, Trent said I didn't have to, but I felt as though I should. I arranged for Carlton and Greene to come and run the yard while I was out.

When the day came, Trent, who had been on duty at the Manor all night, told me that Cavendish and Grace were going to come with us and would pick us up at around ten. A car containing Hayes and Turner followed Cavendish and Grace, and stayed behind us all the way to town. The atmosphere in the car was tense, though that might have just been me as the others were happy to chat, while I stayed silent and stared unseeing out of the window as scenes from Zoe's death played through my mind.

The inquest had been opened by the coroner a few days after Zoe had died, and had to be held because the death was unnatural and caused by violence. Due to my injuries I hadn't attended, but Trent had, although I didn't know it then. Later, he'd told me that it was only to confirm Zoe's identity and the place, time and manner of her death. Because of the circumstances the inquest was then adjourned until a full investigation had been carried out. The coroner had issued an Interim Certificate of the Fact of Death, which had allowed her funeral to take place.

We parked opposite the courthouse, which looked just as I'd imagined a courthouse in a county town would: old red brick, darkly framed windows set in stone surrounds and an arched entrance through which I could see a set of steps disappearing. Trent, Hayes and Turner got out first and surveyed the area before Trent returned to us, indicating it was safe for us all to get out.

As we crossed the cobbled square I saw it – moving in the line of traffic. *A dark blue car, tinted windows obscuring its occupants.* A flashback to the estate's main gate. I'd thought nothing of it then. But now? I tried to get a look at the number plate, but it was side on. By the time we'd reached the kerb it was too far away, and then it was gone. Coincidence? I looked over at Trent. Should I say something? Say what exactly? That I thought I'd just seen a car that might, or might not, have been similar to one I'd seen before? Hardly a compelling reason for a call to action, was it?

We made our way into the building and were directed to the courtroom. My thoughts, full of the issue of the blue car and whether I should say something or not, were interrupted on entering the room as I was alarmed to see there were a few people in there already. I didn't know why that would be. I'd assumed it would be just us, but Trent, seeing me glance anxiously around, whispered that inquests were held in public, and the people in attendance could be nothing to do with our case but there for some other reason that morning. Relieved, I sat down.

The coroner, a thinly drawn man, serious and grey, duly resumed the inquest, running over the basic information before going into further detail. I put my concerns about the blue car out of my mind as he went through the background of Zoe's mental health issues, her marriage and subsequent divorce from Trent, and I wondered if a similar inquest had been held when Eva died. It must have done, only I had been too consumed by grief to deal with it. Something else Alex had done that I should have been thankful for, along with taking legal action against everyone he had felt was responsible. I shivered. Trent's hand closed around mine more tightly as he felt me tremble.

The coroner had moved on, describing how Zoe had absconded from the care she was under and the lead up to the attack on me. They had gleaned a lot of the early information from her doctors. The latter had come from my statement, among others, the forensic and police reports, and finally the post mortem which completed the picture. Numbly I listened to it all, aware of Trent's thumb as it ran soothingly back and forth across my knuckles. The coroner finished his report, then brought the inquest to a close by giving his verdict of lawful killing.

I knew this included lawful self defence so it was the expected verdict, but it seemed a terribly clinical way to deal with the ending of a life. I'd understood the purpose of the inquest was not to determine any liability, apportion guilt or attribute blame, but I still hadn't expected it to be all so – final.

Trent briefly smiled, thought not enough for it to reach his eyes, and I could sense his sadness. A twinge of guilt twisted inside me at the thought that I'd been the cause of it. With no time now for sentiment he indicated we should leave, and before I knew it we were all standing on the steps outside. It was as if I were in a daze. Hayes and Turner stood further away, their backs towards us, on guard. Trent was tense, keen on getting us all, Cavendish in particular, back to the vehicles, but Cavendish halted him for a moment, wanting to make a quick detour to the town council offices where he had some business to deal with.

These offices were next to the courthouse, so we quickly walked down the street before entering a more modern, though less attractive, building than the one we'd just left. As we walked I kept an eye on the traffic. I'd decided if I saw the car again I would say something. Three times could not be a coincidence.

I saw nothing.

Grace and I were left with Turner in the reception area. Cavendish spoke to a lady behind the desk, then he and the others were taken off down a corridor.

As Grace and I made ourselves comfortable, she explained that Cavendish was taking the opportunity of being in town to sort out a problem with the licence for the wedding the following week. He'd offered to license Melton Manor so the event could be hosted there, but at this late stage there'd been a glitch in the paperwork which was causing a delay.

We lapsed back into silence. Turner kept watch by the door, and I noticed how tired and drawn Grace looked.

"How are you dealing with all this, Grace?"

"Oh, you know...probably about as well as you." That was typical of her, always showing empathy for others before thinking of herself.

"I appreciate the thought, but it's not my man that's been threatened."

She turned towards me, thoughtful for a moment before answering.

"You know...you get used to what they do, what they enjoy doing. You worry while they're away and patch them up when they get back. They can't tell you what they've been through and you learn not to ask. But now this seems to have become horribly real, and I have to admit I'm struggling a bit. I'm also not sure if I shall feel better once the children come home, or worse." She looked forlorn, and my heart squeezed in sympathy for her.

"How are they getting on with having bodyguards with them?"

This brought a smile to her lovely face, briefly lighting up her eyes as she replied, "As you can imagine, Reuben loves every minute of it. He thinks it's the coolest thing ever to have a bodyguard at school. Unfortunately, Sophia is absolutely mortified by the whole ordeal, and can't wait for the end of term to come. Fortunately she doesn't have to wait too much longer as they're coming home tomorrow. Which reminds me...we'll have to sort out some riding for them next week? With everything that's been going on, and the wedding coming up, I hadn't thought that far ahead." She swept a tendril of blonde hair off her face and pinned it deftly back in place.

"It would probably be helpful for me to take them off your hands for a while, then."

"Yes it would, although, because of Carlton and Turner having to accompany them, I think their trips to you will have to be curtailed a little as I'm not sure if the boys can be spared for too many hours." Her worried expression was back as she looked anxiously at me, and I felt in her an eagerness to confide her worries. "I know I said I didn't want to leave, and Henry really wanted me to, you know. We had quite a row about it. But he would have sent bodyguards with me if I had gone and that would have weakened the cover here, which seemed illogical." She lapsed into silent worry.

"But now?" I prompted.

"Now...I'm concerned we're putting the children in danger by bringing them home, and I'm wondering if he wasn't right after all."

"Only you can make that decision, Grace. Perhaps you'll know what to do once they get back here, but you know we'll all look after them...and I think you'll feel better once you're all together again." I placed my hand supportively on her upper arm and, although she nodded, I wasn't convinced she believed me. I couldn't imagine anything not being made better by having your child with you.

I looked up to see Trent walking back towards us, closely followed by Cavendish and Hayes.

"Mission accomplished," Trent said. 'We can go home."

Despite the fact that Cavendish thought the most likely place for an attack would be on the estate, I was still considerably more comfortable once we were back through the gates, and even more so when Trent and I had been dropped off at the stables. Having Hayes and Turner watching over us didn't make me feel safer: I felt more anxious and jumpy with them around, and was glad when it was only the two of us again.

Unbelievably, it was still only lunchtime, so I made us some sandwiches and we ate these at the garden table, enjoying another warm and settled summer's day. We only touched briefly on the events of the morning as there didn't seem to be anything else to say on that subject. Instead, we discussed the arrangements for the weekend. Generally, weekends weren't much different for us than any other day of the week, but it was worth running through who was doing what so we could see where we could fit in some time to ourselves.

Unfortunately, although Scott Wade and Lizzie Young could have brought Reuben and Sophia home rather than anyone having to go and get them, Cavendish and Grace had insisted on attending their end-of-term events. This always caused some scheduling problems because they were at different schools, though fortunately these were not too far apart. On this occasion it meant getting to Sophia's school first for an assembly and concert, followed by a sports afternoon at Reuben's school. Trent was going to drive Cavendish and Grace, and take Carlton along for added protection. He made me laugh when he told me of the suggestion made by Reuben that it would be really cool if Cavendish and Grace could arrive in the Apache, and Grace had had to explain that, while that would indeed have been lovely, it was hardly practical as they wouldn't have been able to bring him back with them. At least with the addition of Wade and Young's vehicles there would be plenty of room for both children, plus all their belongings which multiplied over the year.

I could see Trent was concerned about the security issues the day was going to bring, and that he'd feel considerably better once they were all safely back home. We did, though, have something to look forward to in the evening. Stanton and Lawson had decided, in the circumstances, against having stag or hen parties – thank goodness – and instead had opted to have an all-inclusive barbecue which was to be held in the gardens at the Manor – a much better option.

Trent was going to be staying with me for the next couple of nights and would not be on duty at the Manor again until Sunday night. The number of nights he would then have to cover would become fewer as Wade and Young would be back and could help out on the rota, which was just as well as the lack of sleep was taking its toll on him.

After lunch Trent disappeared again to the Manor, and I sorted a few things out then went to do evening stables, and followed this with a visit to the gym for my workout. I came back afterwards to shower and made a start on dinner, which was ready by the time Trent arrived.

I glanced over at him as he came in. "You look exhausted."

"I am." He nodded wearily. "God knows how we're going to cope when harvest starts." It was all he could do to eat, and as soon as he had finished he went to bed.

I went out later with Susie to do the watering and to check on the horses. When I eventually joined Trent I slipped under the duvet, trying not to wake him. He turned towards me, throwing an arm across my body, his leg across one of mine, before resting his head on my chest as he made a deeply contented sighing sound. It made me smile as I lay there, running my fingers through his hair until I dozed off.

We were up early, Trent feeling considerably better with a good night's sleep behind him, and after kissing me goodbye he left to carry out his bodyguard duties for the day. I spent the day in my usual routine, finished off with a trip to the gym, and I was back at the cottage changing when Trent called to let me know they were back and he'd meet me at the barbecue.

Relieved that all had gone well, I went to the Manor in the pickup and headed to the kitchen to see if I could do anything. Finding it bustling with people getting everything ready, I helped carry food out to the garden.

47

Carlton and Cavendish were manning the barbecues already, and I lined up the food for them to start cooking. Carlton handed me a beer, and I took a grateful swig before thanking him for standing in for Trent the other evening; thanks which he brushed off casually before getting back to the serious business of barbecuing, so I wandered off to chat to Greene and Young. I also thanked Greene as I knew she'd instigated Carlton taking on the extra shift. Then Young filled us in on the details of her week guarding Sophia. This had apparently been problematic due to Sophia's reluctance to have Young anywhere near her at any time.

I looked over at the cooks to see they'd been joined by Reuben. Cavendish was trying to teach him the finer points of barbecue cooking, to which he didn't seem to be paying much attention, being more distracted by the actual fire itself. I saw Sophia come out carrying a couple of salads, which she put on the table before running over to say hello.

As I watched her run off again to get a drink I saw Trent arrive at the garden gate, and ridiculously my heart leapt at the sight. I walked across the lawn to meet him, trying to appear grown up and not skip, and greeted him with a kiss and a hug while I breathed him in, content to have him back. He held on to me as he got a drink and we caught up on the day's events.

I noticed Sophia watching us as we talked, and it suddenly occurred to me that she didn't know Trent and I were together, which felt awkward. Both Sophia and Reuben were close to Trent. He was their godfather, and while I didn't imagine Reuben would even notice, let alone be bothered by our relationship, Sophia was that much older and I hoped this wasn't going to be a problem for her.

I turned to Trent. "Sophia...she doesn't know about us. Do you think..."

"I know what you're going to say," he broke in. "I'll have a word with her." He headed towards the kitchen door, following Sophia.

The pair of them emerged a little while later, both carrying baskets of rolls and looking as if they were in the middle of a serious conversation. Sophia's eyes darted over to me a couple of times as I watched them. Depositing their baskets on the table, Trent reached over to get Sophia a drink and she grinned at him then, looking over at me, she gave me a quick, shy-looking wave before turning and going back to the kitchen.

Trent came over and met my enquiring look with a smile. "She's fine about you being my girlfriend. She was actually quite pleased, just surprised she hadn't already heard about it."

Soon everyone was there and the food was ready, so we tucked in, eating far more than necessary. Afterwards we sat on the grass, feeling full and as if we couldn't move for a while, enjoying the company until Reuben came charging past us, clearly on a mission.

"What are you up to?" Trent shouted after the disappearing boy. Reuben called back breathlessly that he was off to get a bat, we were to have a game.

My heart sank a little as Trent dragged me to my feet. I hoped we weren't talking cricket. We rounded up the others and went out into the parkland at the front of the Manor. Reuben appeared holding aloft his baseball bat, and we played girls against boys, fiercely competitive, until we lost the light and couldn't see the ball any more. It was one of those fun impromptu evenings that you never want to end.

As we all wandered back to the garden, I was pretty relaxed. This was what we'd needed: a bit of fun to chase away the worries for a while. We went to fill up on more drink and summer pudding, thereby undoing all the good work done by playing baseball. And although Trent and I left around midnight, it looked like some were set to party on into the night.

# Chapter 5

Although the security level on the estate had been heightened, the following week was going to revolve around preparations for the wedding due to taken place on the Saturday, but first, on the Monday, we had to get through Zoe's interment. Despite the fact she'd attacked me, I'd felt terribly sad for Zoe. She wasn't in her right mind when she'd done it, and I knew she must have loved Trent very much, so I'd been the one to suggest interring her ashes in the same churchyard as Eva. I knew how Trent had felt about her, and I thought our loved ones should be together. Trent had taken me up on the idea and had arranged for a small service of committal to be held by the vicar there.

I knew Cavendish and Grace were going to go with us, but Trent announced the day before that Carlton and Greene were also going to come. Trent knew I'd told Greene about Eva, so had thought it was best if they came along as additional security as it wouldn't raise too many questions. I was still getting my head round the fact that Greene was qualified to be taking on a security detail.

We travelled in two vehicles and, though a passenger, I kept my eyes on the road, peeled for any sign of the blue car. We got to Crowbridge shortly before noon when the service was due to start. As we entered the churchyard I glanced across to where Eva lay, as I always did, but then we took a different path and crossed to the other side of the church and the garden of remembrance. The vicar welcomed everyone and greeted me kindly, asking how I was and pressing my hand between his two. It brought back the memory of him doing the same thing before

Eva's funeral, and I had to bite my lip hard to stop the tears. Then we gathered around the hole where the box containing Zoe's ashes would be buried, and Trent gripped my hand as the vicar spoke kind, well chosen and thoughtful words of Zoe, her life and her achievements. He had done his homework, though I could hear Trent's influence throughout the words he spoke. After the bleakness of the funeral and the impersonal nature of the inquest, this was what was needed. I was pleased for Trent that we'd taken this opportunity to stand together on a beautiful summer's day and give thanks for her life.

Once the service was finished and the vicar had gone into the church, Trent bent down to the flowers we were going to leave with Zoe and took a couple out of the arrangement before handing them to me. He took hold of my free hand, threading his fingers in between mine, an indication that he was coming with me. I looked at the flowers, then at the others and asked if they could give us a moment or two. There was a hesitation, and it didn't appear to have been planned, but Carlton, glancing at the others, cleared his throat.

"We were wondering if we could come with you, Em?"

My throat tightened and I blinked away tears. Not risking speech, I simply nodded. Trent and I led the others round the church to where my angel lay, and as we stopped at the foot of the grave Cavendish and Grace joined us, though Greene and Carlton stood further away, their backs to us, keeping watch. Cavendish, next to me, put his arm round my shoulders, hugging me to him. Grace moved past him and wrapped her arms around me. Trent released my hand so I could return the hug, but as she pulled back I saw her try to wipe her tears away before I saw them.

"I'm so sorry," she mumbled, "it's just that I can't imagine..." Her voice tailed off.

"I know...It's okay," I reassured her. Looking at the flowers I held, I broke the moment, giving Grace a chance to turn to Cavendish for comfort as I went to add these flowers to the others I'd left there the previous week.

"I think we'll head back to the cars and give you some time," Cavendish said as he and Grace turned and walked away. Greene and Carlton fell in behind them. I rejoined Trent and stood facing him as he took my hands in his, pulling me closer.

"This is the first time I've been here," he murmured. "Are you okay?"

"I'm fine actually. It feels good to be here with you, with our friends. It's good that they know. It's not like I want everyone to know, but those closest to us...it seems right somehow." He nodded before leaning in to kiss me, and he asked if I wanted him to leave me to spend some time alone at the graveside. I knew he'd be anxious to get back to Cavendish, to get him back home, so I said no, and after turning to say goodbye quietly to Eva, we left together.

Although activity on the estate over the next few days escalated, my little world remained largely the same as I was not involved with the wedding preparations. I was therefore pleased when Trent arrived one evening later in the week to ask if I wanted to go with him to the tree house. He'd been sent on a mission to retrieve the fairy lights which, it was thought, had last been seen there. I jumped at the chance, having wanted to explore the tree house ever since discovering it the previous year.

Susie and I had found a new path through the woods which opened up into an area cleared of all undergrowth, but with three large trees growing up out of it. I'd looked up in astonishment as, high in the branches and built between these trees, was a huge tree house. A set of wooden stairs climbed up from the woodland floor, spiralling around one tree trunk before leading to the front door. There were three more or less circular rooms that blended together where they touched. The tiled roof of each room was conical, the walls weather-boarded. I'd run up the steps to see if I could see inside, but had been disappointed to find the door was solid, all the windows closed with internal shutters, and I could see no more. It looked like more than just a tree house for children to play in, though, and I'd wondered who used it. Reluctantly I'd gone back down the steps and carried on with my walk, imagining how wonderful it would be to live there.

We drove past the main gate and back into the woodland the other side, before turning off the road and stopping eventually at the end of a woodchip path. Following this path between the trees we came into the clearing and climbed the steps. Trent opened the door and held it for me to enter. He folded back the shutters to some of the windows to give enough light to see by. My eyes widened. This was far beyond any tree house I could ever have imagined. We'd walked straight into the kitchen, which was big enough to take everything a kitchen needed. The floor units fitted the curve of the walls; the windows filled in the space above. There was a small bare wooden table in the centre of the room with two chairs, all in a white Shaker style.

Two doors led off the kitchen, one to a beautiful, cosy snug where a large, curved, comfortable-looking settee hugged the wall. I could imagine the bliss of curling up to read a book in front of the small wood-burning stove. This seemed incongruous in a tree house, but it fitted in perfectly with the no-expense-spared design. The other opened onto the bedroom where I found Trent, who was going through the contents of a built-in storage cupboard. I left him to it as I carried on my explorations into the bathroom. The whole tree house was a perfect fully-functioning little retreat. Trent had told me that was what

Cavendish and Grace used it for. I rejoined him in the bedroom and sat on the edge of the bed, looking over at him as he suddenly appeared to find what he'd been looking for and started taking out bundles of lights and placing them on the floor beside him.

I coughed gently to attract his attention, and when he looked round at me I smiled and raised my eyebrows at him, drumming my fingers on the bed beside me. He returned my smile and I thought for a moment he would come to join me, but instead he carried on with the job in hand. Once he had all the lights out of the cupboard I tried to attract his attention again, and this time succeeded in getting him to come over to the bed. He bent down, planting a kiss softly on my cheek before lifting me up into a standing position. I looked at him and I know confusion must have shown on my face.

"You're turning me down?" This was a first, and a bit of a blow to my confidence, I had to admit. He put his hands on my hips and studied me thoughtfully before replying.

"Not turning you down exactly, more...putting you off for a bit."

I frowned, narrowing my eyes at him in suspicion. "That's not like you, what's wrong?"

"Nothing's wrong, it's not the right time, that's all." And he kissed me gently as if to mollify me. I felt as if I'd been given the brush-off as he turned to start gathering up the lights, urging me to do the same. We carried them all to the truck and put them carefully in the back before driving off. I was quiet, feeling a little hurt and bewildered by Trent's rejection, but when we got to the Manor the place was buzzing and I spent the next couple of hours with everyone else, helping to decorate the Manor with the lights. It was good to have others around to dilute a bit of the tension between us. Trent didn't explain or even mention what had happened at the tree house, and when

55

we got home he was as amorous as ever and I ended up shrugging off the incident as being one of those things, like he'd said...not the right time.

The day of the wedding dawned. The service was going to be mid-afternoon, so my plan was to get the horses ridden and then turned out so I could get the stables ready for the evening and have time to shower and change. Trent was going to pick me up in time to get to the service. At some point I'd pop back to finish off the horses before returning to the party for the evening.

Sophia and Reuben had been to the stables a couple of times in the last week, but it had always been a bit rushed, partly because everyone was so busy with the wedding preparations, and partly because Carlton and Turner had to accompany the children and I felt awkward keeping them hanging around for too long. This meant that there hadn't been much time for the children to renew their skills in the saddle. I was hoping once the wedding was out of the way the children might be able to spend a bit more time here.

I'd restricted my riding to the estate grounds since the threat against Cavendish had been made, mainly because it was so difficult to get out of the gates, but also because Trent had asked me to do this. Though I didn't always do what he asked, on this occasion I didn't want to be too far away in case something happened and I needed to return to the stables quickly. This morning was a glorious one; the sun beat down, but there was a light breeze which took the edge off the heat. I chose my routes so I had a chance to pass by the Manor and see what was going on in the build up.

I knew from Trent that the security for the day was proving to be a bit of a headache, mostly because of the number of guests arriving from off the estate. Stanton and Lawson had fifty or so family and friends coming, and it had taken some arranging to get them all either to stay at or agree to be picked up from a large hotel in the nearby town so that they could all travel in one coach. Unbeknown to them all, the guests had already been security cleared and a system had been set up so that each one could be checked on to the coach and kept tabs on throughout the day, before being checked back on to the coach at the end of the celebrations and escorted off the estate again. This all had to be done as surreptitiously as possible so as not to raise any suspicions among the guests that anything was amiss, not only for their sake but mostly for Stanton and Lawson. Everyone wanted their big day to go off as smoothly and naturally as possible. Trent was hoping that the estate would come across as highly efficient rather than anally security conscious.

As I headed back on Monty, my second ride of the day, I rode up the main drive and, turning right towards the stables, a glint of reflected sunlight caught my eye. I looked over, through the intricate wrought iron of the gates – a car, dark blue, stationary on the road. Spots of sparkling chrome had alerted me to its presence. As it paused for a moment longer, I imagined the eyes behind the tinted windows making a connection with mine as the hairs on the back of my neck rose and my skin prickled. It drove off and, knowing what I now needed to do, I returned quickly to the stables and leapt off Monty, glad to be able to take off the back protector Trent had bought me – and insisted I wear.

I hesitated as I reached for my phone. Should I tell him now? He was busy travelling back with the wedding guests, and I knew he wouldn't want them to be alerted to anything being wrong. Was it so important that it couldn't wait until he got back? It was hardly as if the estate was actually being stormed, was it?

I sponged down Monty and Zodiac as I mulled over my indecision at what I should do, then took them out to the field where they joined Regan and Benjy, immediately dropping to the ground to roll. Deciding my news could wait until he got here I returned to the yard, cleared out the stables, made up the beds and filled the hay nets and water buckets ready for the evening. Once I was finished I went into the cottage, disturbing a sleeping Susie who was whacked out after joining me on the first ride.

I leapt in the shower, washed my hair, then went downstairs and made myself a sandwich for lunch before getting ready. I'd bought a simple linen sheath dress in cornflower blue which I squeezed into after drying my hair. I slipped on the pair of heels I was going to risk, thinking that if necessary I could always change into some a little lower and more comfortable when I came back to do the horses. Trent called to say he'd arrived back with the coach, and with everyone now safely on the estate he'd be with me in a couple of minutes.

I went downstairs, checking Susie had all she needed before locking her in for the afternoon, then went out to meet Trent who was driving into the yard. He jumped out of the truck and whistled appreciatively, his eyes lighting up as he came to greet me. Don't tell him right away, I thought, at least say "Hello" first.

"You look fabulous," he murmured as he wrapped his arms around me, his hands following the contours of the dress, and my body.

"Looking pretty good yourself," I responded. He was in a sharp navy suit, crisp white shirt and navy patterned tie. His lips found mine as he kissed me hungrily, but then, glancing at his watch, he exhaled in frustration.

"Much as I want to take you into the cottage and peel you back out of that dress, there's no time for that now."

You're going to ruin this good mood of his, I thought sadly as I shook my head at him in mock disbelief. "You are incorrigible."

"I know, but I'm kind of hoping you wouldn't have me any other way." And he grinned his irresistible grin before leading me round to the truck's passenger side. As he opened the door and helped me up in my less than practical outfit, his hand lingered a little too long on my backside.

"Steady," I said, smiling as I heard him chuckle softly behind me. He was in a playful mood, which was good, all things considered, and I hated the fact that what I was about to say was going to bring an end to that.

As he got in the cab, I turned to him. "Trent, before we leave I need to tell you something." And I told him about the three sightings I'd had. When I finished, I sat back. The evidence for suspicion still seemed fairly thin to me, and I wasn't sure if I was about to be scoffed at or taken seriously.

We sat where we were as Trent put calls through to Sharpe in the office and Cavendish. He sent out a text to all – we were upgraded to a state of high alert. I was taken very seriously.

Then we drove to the Manor. It was too late to make any changes to the wedding, so it had been decided we would press ahead with the plans already in place and we pulled into the courtyard where I could see the coach parked up to the side. I could feel Trent's tension as we passed through the stone arch into the garden, our feelings incongruous to the wonderfully relaxed summery scene that greeted us. Groups of guests were scattered across the lawn, enjoying a pre-wedding drink. The marquee that had been erected to hold the service and reception was at the end of the lawn closest to the main house. The sides had been removed, showing rows of chairs, each swathed in cream fabric finished off with a decorative bow to the rear. An aisle ran between them up the centre of the marquee. The roof was lined, and large flower arrangements had been placed in each corner, with two further arrangements marking each side of the place where the couple would be saying their vows.

Trent and I made our way across the lawn, Trent's hand never leaving the small of my back. I remembered all the reasons why it was such a pain to wear heels in the first place, and to a wedding in particular, as I struggled to avoid them sinking into the lawn. Acting as if we hadn't a care in the world, we took a glass of champagne from the tray offered to us by Sophia in a pale pink dress, the bodice embroidered with small flowers. She was looking very pretty, and blushed when we told her so. We circulated with the guests, chatting to those we knew, introducing ourselves to those we didn't. Trent discretely took each of the estate staff he came across to one side, making sure they were geared up for the day ahead.

He then disappeared for a while to the office, and on rejoining the gathering told me quietly he'd had a look at the CCTV footage from the main gate. It had added nothing to what I'd been able to tell him other than how long they'd been sitting there taking in the details of the new security around the entrance.

We made our way across to a nervous-looking Stanton to offer our best wishes, and I hoped he hadn't been made aware of the high alert situation as he introduced us to his brother and best man, Michael. We talked to them for a few minutes, then moved on as others came up to talk to them. A short while later Stanton and Michael started moving through the guests and towards the marquee. As they reached the edge of the crowd they turned, and Michael announced the service would soon start and urged everyone to find a seat. The guests started moving and gradually the marquee filled up. Trent and I remained where we were for a moment, and when we were alone Trent took out his phone and made a couple of calls to those responsible for the security and surveillance over the estate. When he had checked that all was well, we took up our places in the marquee. But I knew he was worrying –

if it all kicked off now, how would it go down with all these innocent people around?

The registrar was already in place, standing between the flower arrangements at the front and chatting to Stanton and Michael. Clearly he'd said something funny as they both chuckled lightly, and I could see their tension dissipate a little with their smiles.

The music started, coming from hidden speakers in the corners of the ceiling of the marquee. It was a classical piece, which needless to say I was unfamiliar with, and we all stood. Stanton looked down the aisle, his face lighting up as he saw Lawson on the arm of her father. A lump came to my throat as I watched him escort his daughter. Being an orphan and never having known my father, I'd always found this ritual deeply poignant in a way you can only appreciate when it's something you can never experience.

We sat and listened as the registrar guided Stanton and Lawson through the service. They'd written their own vows, which I thought brave, and they were sweet and meaningful. Trent sat with his arm along the back of my chair, his fingers still and light on my upper arm. We were at the back and I could see all the guests. It amazed me how many of the people here were family members. Parents, grandparents, brothers, sisters, aunts, uncles and cousins from both sides of the family. It intrigued me how large and yet how close these two families were that were being brought together into one. A stark contrast to Trent and me, neither of us having any family, isolated in the crowd.

The ceremony ended with a kiss accompanied by spontaneous applause, and we all stood as the couple walked back down the aisle, confetti thrown in celebration. Another round of drinks was to be served in the garden with canapés, and this was my cue to leave and get the horses finished off for the evening. Due to my stupid shoes, Trent said he'd run me back to the yard then take a lap round the estate to check all was in order before picking me up again.

We returned to the party later, me having changed my shoes, and I made my way to the kitchen as I was helping to get the food ready for the reception. Although I was involved in finishing off some of the preparation, mostly I was carrying it through to the ballroom. We were going to serve it buffet style for everyone to eat at tables which had been set up under the marquee, but which also spilled out on to the lawn. It had been decided that we'd operate in a similar way to how the ball had been run earlier in the year. We'd all pitch in to help, which would cut down the numbers of outsiders that would have to come on to the estate. Therefore, while we'd been gone a group had set up the tables and chairs, then the tables had been beautifully laid and decorated with floral arrangements incorporating candles which would be lit as the evening progressed. Part of the marquee floor had been left clear for dancing, and a band was setting up at the far end.

To the uninitiated among us the celebrations appeared like those of any country wedding. To those in the know it was hard to miss the comings and goings of the staff as they rotated security detail, the muttered asides when reporting back that all was quiet, and I knew all were holding their breath, hoping that tonight was not going to be the night.

The buffet table was long and fully laden, and Michael started organising everyone to come through before taking their allotted seats. We served ourselves last and took our seats, and the wine flowed for our guests, though I noticed those from the estate abstaining due to the duties they still had to fulfil.

The speeches were mercifully short, albeit entertaining, and for me, at least, very informative. I found out that Stanton was a doctor, not a gardener as I'd believed. He had served as an army medic, and it had been on active service that he'd met Lawson who was, in fact, a qualified nurse and not a farm hand. As this was revealed to me I looked over at Trent, who raised his eyebrows innocently as if he too were surprised.

The cake was cut and served as dessert as the band started to play. Trent took my hand and led me away from the crowd to a quiet corner further up the garden, and although the music being played was upbeat Trent drew me closer to him and we moved slowly to our own tune.

"Go on, then," he said.

"Go on with what?"

"With all those questions that are bursting out of you."

"Ah, you know me too well..." I hesitated. "So how does it work then? Stanton and Lawson are both working here in different occupations. Do their families know they've opted out?"

"They haven't opted out. They're both still what they qualified as. They're part of our team. Stanton is our only doctor, but we have others qualified as nurses. They all work enough hours at the local hospital to keep them qualified and their skills up to date – actually, they specialise in accident and emergency medicine as that's most useful for us." He paused to look at me for a moment before continuing, grinning as he wound me up, "With the number of visits you've had to the hospital it's surprising you haven't bumped into any of them there."

I ignored his little joke. "So they're what? Living some sort of double life?"

"I guess so. People are here for a variety of reasons. Some of the older ones had retired from the forces but weren't quite able to completely let it go. Here, they can live a gentler life but keep their skills up with the chance that they may still be needed. Others, the younger ones...at least some of them have had...some sort of bad experience, in the field usually, that has set them back. They have either been recommended to come here, or have requested the transfer themselves to give them a bit of breathing space or recovery time before deciding what to do next. Some we have actively recruited and they are here on secondment from the forces for a period of time. It all depends on the individuals' circumstances, but basically all here are not what they seem to the outside world."

I thought on this for a moment. There was one person who was different to the others.

"What's Turner's story then? If I'm allowed to know, that is?"

Turner had stood out from the other boys right from the start. He was very young, still only just twenty, and although he'd filled out a little in the year I'd known him through trying to keep up with the others at the gym, he had a way to go to catch up with their physiques.

"He is a little different. He'd shown great potential in the Navy and earned his wings in record time, but was struggling with accepting the discipline that was expected of him. He'd got himself into a few fights due to his hotheadedness, but was ill-equipped to deal with them. An old contact got in touch and asked us to take him on for a while. He pilots a small transport aircraft we use when several of us are deploying, or we need certain equipment."

I hadn't realised they had anything other than the Apache.

"I suppose you were sympathetic because he reminded you of you." I remembered Trent surprising me when he'd revealed how he'd struggled in a similar fashion when he was younger.

"I suppose so. Anyway, here he can develop at his own speed, and once he feels ready he can go back to his unit." I could feel Trent's attention wandering as he looked across the garden towards the marquee, and I knew I'd got all the information from him that I was likely to get for a while. I knew he was thinking about the security issues of the evening, so I nodded as he said, "We'd better be rejoining the party."

The band was in full swing and the dance floor heaving as we wandered back across the grass, walking up to Cavendish and Grace who were watching from the sidelines. My head was full of everything I'd recently learnt about the estate and those on it. I had lived here over a year believing all these people around me were gardeners, farm hands, cleaners and the like. They lived this quiet life, worked on a beautiful estate doing these steady jobs when in fact they were all militarily trained and, it seemed, just waiting for that training to be put to good use.

It appeared their time had come.

The band had come to the end of a song, changing the tempo into something slower, much to the relief of some of those on the dance floor. Some left while others joined. I took Trent's hand in an attempt to coax him on to the floor. Instantly I could feel him tense.

"I can't...I'm sorry...I've got to go and check on...a few things." As excuses went, he didn't carry this one off well. His words stilted and false. His hand tightened on mine as Carlton joined our little group, he and Greene fresh from the dance floor, though Greene was disappearing in the opposite direction.

Trent cleared his throat. "Why don't you have a dance with Carlton? He's unoccupied at the moment..." His discomfort was almost palpable, and made worse by the group's reaction. Cavendish swiftly asked Grace to dance, not waiting for an answer as she was only too happy to be given a way out of the awkwardness. Trent, Carlton and I were left, and I'd been so completely taken by surprise I had no chance to hide my look of astonishment as my eyes flicked across Carlton's face. His eyebrows lifted in a similar response to mine. I looked at Trent, bewildered by his out-of-character behaviour.

While I took longer to get my reaction under control. Carlton didn't waste a second, holding his hand out to me as Trent gave an imperceptible nod in my direction, keen for me to accept the offer. Confused, I took Carlton's hand, accepting the situation as his mouth formed an "only too happy to oblige" smile.

As we walked the few paces to the dance floor, I glanced back over my shoulder to see Trent's eyes darkening as they fixed on mine. My initial surprise over, I now knew what he was doing and I knew what it would be costing him. Carlton pulled me closer, and taking the opportunity I looked over his shoulder, only to find Trent had gone.

"Relax, Em." I heard Carlton's quiet words close to my ear before he pulled back to look at me. I smiled unsteadily, trying to prove to him that I could smile, willing my body to do as he suggested. But a memory was stirred by being this close to Carlton, and as our eyes met I was instantly transported back to the night in the stable yard, before Trent had intervened in what might have been. This memory immediately intensified my discomfort. Carlton's expression was serious, his eyes fixed on mine. I didn't think his thoughts were that far from my own.

Then, leaving me in no doubt, he murmured, "Ancient history now, Em...we've both moved on and we need to get more...we need to be more comfortable with each other, and with the way things are now."

I've never felt more grateful, more relieved, or more instantly relaxed as at that moment when we both grinned, broadly and ridiculously, at each other.

"Thank God we got that over with," I replied.

"Awkward, wasn't it?" He grinned as I nodded in agreement, laughing lightly as we continued to move slowly round the floor, smoothly now, comfortably. Cocking his head to one side, he continued, "So...what's he up to?"

"He did take me by surprise, but I know what it's all about now. It's because of our row. There was a situation...I won't elaborate, but he's trying to show me he's not possessive."

"Ah, I wondered what it had been about." He looked thoughtful. "I'm still surprised he invited me to dance with you, particularly after our 'moment'." And he grinned as I grimaced at the reminder.

"He tends to be all or nothing," I said. "You happened to be there, and by choosing you it shows he's trying particularly hard to prove something to me."

"I hope you appreciate the gesture."

The song had come to an end. We wandered out of the marquee and back towards the entrance to the kitchen. I thought I'd offer my services, and Carlton indicated he was going to the office to check in on the surveillance team. I was in time to help take platters of cheese and baskets of biscuits out to the guests in an attempt to help soak up some of the alcohol they'd imbibed.

It seemed no time at all before we were all standing in front of the Manor sending the newlyweds off on their honeymoon, and as I stood out of the way behind all the family, Trent appeared silently beside me. Goodbyes were said, the bride and groom left and their guests returned to the partying – we didn't move.

Heeding Carlton's words, I wondered how to let Trent know I appreciated the effort he'd made, and thinking how to go about this made me feel awkward with him. I could sense his eyes on me, watching me, and before I could find something appropriate to say, he spoke, "Good dance?"

"Yes...thank you." I turned to him, putting my hand on his chest, then, wanting to encourage him, I met his eyes. "But it wasn't you." A flicker of suppressed satisfaction passed across his face. "I appreciate it, Trent...it means a lot."

He shrugged as if it was nothing, when I knew that for him it was everything. "I'm aiming to turn my possessiveness into protectiveness which I hope you will be able to accept."

I didn't like to dampen his enthusiasm by mentioning that I didn't need protecting either. Graciously accept the small steps, I told myself. So I smiled at him as, stepping closer, his arms closed around me, and we stood for a while enjoying the peace of what was now a late summer's night.

The party wound down a short while later when the more than merry wedding guests were rounded up and shepherded back on to the coach, where they enjoyed a raucous farewell. As the coach disappeared from view up the lane, a relieved silence fell over the estate workers left behind. With an almost grim determination we turned to the task of dismantling the marquee and clearing away all signs of the celebrations. It was clear the party was over.

# Chapter 6

The mood on the estate changed after the wedding. Even though I was distanced by being at the stables, the more serious air pervading the atmosphere reached me, probably transmitted via Trent, and I felt edgy. I went to a couple of briefings at the Manor where we found out a little more about the members of the organisation we were being threatened by, and had the opportunity to view the few, mostly grainy, photographs on record of them. Out of the Polzin brothers, it seemed as though only the youngest, Anatoly, involved himself in any direct action, the others taking more organisational roles. Cavendish and Trent had come up against him before, along with one of the gang's particularly brutal henchmen, Orlov. We were kept updated on any available intel (I was also learning the lingo) but it wasn't much. Despite my sightings of the blue car we still had no idea how, when or even if they were coming.

As a distraction I was pleased to have the children over on a couple of days to ride, and we stayed in the arena which made it easier for Carlton and Turner to be able to keep an eye on them. Towards the end of the week, however, they were getting itchy feet, and as Grace was also coming over to ride we thought we'd hack out.

I mapped out the route I would take with Carlton and Turner and planned it so they'd be able to follow us via the lanes, and although they wouldn't quite be able to keep us in sight all the time, they'd be near enough to get to us if needed.

Trent had come back for lunch, and met Grace, Sophia and Reuben in the yard as he was leaving. Reuben's face grimaced with distaste as Trent kissed me goodbye. Sophia had obviously spread the news to him as he didn't seem surprised at our display of affection, only disgusted.

The horses had been particularly bothered by flies over the last week and I'd changed their routine to keep them in during the day and out overnight, so they were already in when we went to get them ready. We set off half an hour later. Carlton and Turner followed us out of the yard in the pickup and trailed along behind us until we turned into the trees, and we lost sight of them as the lane drew them away from us. It felt good to be out; the weather was fine and warm, and it was difficult to believe the threat hanging over the estate was real. Grace appeared pent-up and tense, which was perhaps not surprising, and as we walked our horses side by side, the children following along behind giggling about something, I quietly asked how she was coping.

She shrugged, sighing deeply before she replied, keeping her voice low so the children wouldn't hear. "You were quite right, I do feel better having the children with us, but other than that I feel a bit useless. I'm worried for Cavendish, but he seems confident that all the plans they've put in place will be enough..." She hesitated. "But what if they're not? What if he gets taken from us? I feel so scared...and, frankly, completely out of my depth surrounded by all these people who know what they're doing."

I could understand her misgivings and sympathised with her. I'd done my own share of feeling inadequate over the predicament we'd found ourselves in. I also got the feeling she'd not said this out loud before, and hoped that perhaps she saw I was in a similar position, which was why she'd taken the chance to offload.

"I know what you mean with feeling out of your depth, Grace, but you bring your own skills to this situation. I'm somewhat separated from what's going on, but Trent has told me about all the organisation you've been involved with, sorting the staff and supplies, organising rotas – even manning the surveillance, I've heard."

She laughed at this and smiled across at me. "Did you hear what happened as I was being briefed by Sharpe in the office?" Although I had heard, I shook my head, wanting her to tell me; to make me laugh; to make her relax. She went on eagerly, "Sharpe was showing me how the screens worked where you could swap from one camera angle to another and so on, when up popped the view of the back courtyard, and there were Hayes and Young in a compromising position behind one of the pickups. Sharpe was horrified that I was there to witness it, and though I tried to take it seriously I couldn't help laughing. I laughed even more as she tried to call both of them, but they were so caught up in the moment they ignored their phones. I think that was what she found most annoying." Grace was having to wipe her tears of laughter away as she told me this, and as I laughed along with her I could imagine how mortified Sharpe would have been. Trent had told me the story as it had been regaled to him by Sharpe, and her indignation at having her calls ignored when the estate was meant to be in a state of high alert was clear. You had to admit she had a point.

As our laughter eased we became aware of the giggling growing louder behind us, and whisperings between the children as they appeared to be goading each other into song. I heard "Grayson and Trent, sitting in a tree, k-i-s-s-i-n-g" followed by more giggles. Grace and I looked at each other before joining in their laughter.

"Right, come on, you lot, let's get you working so you have less energy to tease me with." And we moved into a brisk trot. Everyone more relaxed already, and as I heard the acceleration of the pickup along the road a short distance from us, I felt as settled as could be expected at the moment.

We covered a good distance round the estate, taking the opportunity to be out for a couple of hours, then headed back to the stables at a walk to cool the horses down. Although we'd spied the pickup a couple of times during the ride, it was currently out of sight. Carlton had done a good job of not drawing too much attention to it as we were trying to make everything as normal as possible for the sake of the children.

I was at the rear of the group, having put Sophia and Reuben in charge of leading the way home, and I took the opportunity to have a look around, enjoying the chance to appreciate the beauty of the woodland that was so easy to take for granted when you saw it every day. As I checked on the children ahead I felt an uneasy prickling on the back of my neck. I'd missed something. Nothing appeared to have changed around us, but I knew there was something out of place. I could feel it but couldn't pinpoint the source.

Stopping Regan, I scanned the scenery again, but this time more slowly, trying to spot the inconsistency that had led to this heightened sense of awareness. Grace pulled up ahead and looked back at me, frowning as she wondered what I was up to. I could see nothing around me and checked again, twisting in the saddle to look further through the woodland, right through as far as the estate wall, only partly visible between the trees. Then I saw it – two black strips stretching across the top of the wall – something out of place.

I indicated to Grace to carry on and said I'd catch them up in a minute. I turned off the track and headed for the wall. This part of the wall dipped down into a hollow then rose again, and I rode to the highest point, pulling Regan tight up against the wall so he was parallel to it. Standing in the stirrups I leant over as far as I could to try to see what was on the other side. I could see the black strips were bars ending in hooks that curled over the top of the wall and gripped the underside of the overhang. Peering over I could see the black rungs of the ladder they held in place.

They'd chosen a good point to enter. This part of the wall was well hidden from the road that passed above it, the land falling away into the hollow which meant you couldn't see anything unless you stopped your car and got out to look for it. I rode down to the bottom of the hill, thinking that until this moment I'd only thought of the threat as being something that might happen one day, and now it was suddenly horribly real. I halted a little short of the area below the metal bars and had a quick look at the ground, searching for clues as to whether someone had already climbed over the wall. It was difficult to tell. There was little grass in this shady area. The ground was covered with leaf litter and small twigs, but being in a hollow the soil was soft, slow to dry out even in the heat of summer. As I leant down over Regan's withers to look closer, I could definitely see indentations. No clear footprints, though. No clue as to how many had passed that way.

I sat up quickly, looking around, immediately feeling eyes upon me. But seeing no one as I scanned the woods, I pushed Regan on, hurrying back through the trees to catch up with the others who were nearing the end of the path and about to come out on to the road. As I did so I pulled out my phone and called Trent.

"Someone's on the estate," I said, my heart pounding. Questions followed, details were requested and answered, and my replies were passed on to others around him. I gathered he was in the office. I pictured the room, with probably several of them scanning all the camera angles looking for the intruders. By the time I'd given him all the information I had I'd caught up with the others, and exchanged a look with Grace that told her all she needed to know.

Trent spoke, clear and concise. "Get everyone back to the stables, Grayson. Update Carlton and Turner, and keep Grace and the children in the cottage until we know more. Understood?"

"Understood," I repeated, and ended the call. At that moment I heard an engine rev up and glimpsed the pickup accelerating away down the lane and away from the stables – that was not what I'd been expecting.

Grace took the lead, trying to act casually so as not to alarm the children. I stayed behind, and as we rode out on to the lane where I'd been expecting to see the pickup, there was only Carlton standing in the road waiting for us. The gateway to the stables was within sight, and I was anxious to get everyone into the yard as if it represented some place of safety. I met Carlton's eye and he knew immediately something had happened. As I passed him I leant down and spoke quietly.

"Carlton, go ahead to the stables. Check if the cottage is okay. Susie will tell you all you need to know. Get the door open and come back out to help me with the horses." Carlton nodded and I saw him disappear through the gates. We followed him, and as we entered the yard he was already coming back out of the cottage, giving me a surreptitious thumb-up.

I leapt off Regan and took Monty's reins from Grace. Carlton came over to take Zodiac and Benjy, which I knew would bring protests from the children as they were used to dealing with their own ponies. Needing to distract them, I invited Sophia and Reuben to have an ice-cream and asked Grace to show them where they were. Grace shepherded them inside while Carlton and I untacked the horses, cleaned them off and led them straight out to the paddock as quickly as we could, speaking under our breath to each other as we did so.

"Where are Turner and the pickup?" I asked.

"It started misfiring and I didn't want it breaking down on us, so I sent him to the farm to get one of the mechanics to have a look at it."

"Mechanics?" More new information for me to process.

"Porter and a couple of the others, Royal Engineers" was Carlton's matter of fact reply. Of course. I shrugged to myself as I filled him in on my discovery and Trent's instructions. We left the horses and headed back to the cottage, having a good look up into the trees surrounding us as we went. Carlton went straight through to the sitting room, and I saw him checking out the windows that faced on to the road as he took out his phone to call Porter for an update on the pickup repairs.

I sat at the table watching Reuben and Sophia as they ate their ice-creams. Sophia had some chocolate round her mouth, and Reuben's was spread down his chin as well. They watched us silently. They weren't stupid. They knew something was up; their mother's badly disguised agitation was hard to ignore, and I didn't think it would be long before we'd have to tell them what was going on.

I heard the low murmur of Carlton's voice, too low to hear what was being said, and then he appeared in the doorway, caught my eye and indicated for me to join him. I followed him through the sitting room into the office, where he announced bluntly, "Turner never reached the farm."

Oh crap. A sick feeling turned my stomach. Before I had the chance to say anything Carlton's phone vibrated, and as he answered the call he mouthed the word "Trent" to me. I nodded, waiting for the update which sounded curt, mirroring Carlton's perfunctory replies.

When he hung up he said, "The pickup's been found driven off the road in the woods between here and the farm. Driver's side door open, no sign of a disturbance, no sign of Turner."

I looked at him. "What do we do?"

"We sit tight and see what develops."

I nodded, then went back to the kitchen. Carlton followed. Grace had cleaned up the children and was busy getting the kettle on for tea. I sent the children through to watch some television while we organised supper. None of us felt like eating, but we took the opportunity to update Grace while we made sandwiches. She didn't say anything, but busied herself searching my kitchen to add crisps, fruit and cake to the supper, which she eventually served in an overly bright manner as a picnic on the floor of the sitting room. I thought her behaviour would ensure that if the children didn't think something was up before, they surely would now. Carlton kept a look out of the window as Grace passed him food, encouraging all of us to eat something, and in doing so indicated silently that she knew we could have a long wait ahead of us.

I cleared up in the kitchen as Carlton stuck to his position by the front windows. As the light faded he drew the curtains and kept watch through the small gap he'd left in them. The lights were off; the only light flickered from the television, and as time wore on and Grace struggled to find anything that would hold the children's interest, eventually that was turned off too. They'd done well holding back their questions, but I now heard Sophia's soft voice asking her mother what was going on. In a speech she'd probably been rehearsing since entering the cottage, I listened as Grace restricted her explanation to the fact that some people had been spotted on the estate that shouldn't be there, and we were to sit tight until they'd been apprehended.

Simultaneously Carlton's and my phones indicated an incoming text. We glanced at each other as we checked the message.

"Turner's duress password has been used for three vehicles to enter the estate."

I closed my eyes. What'd they done to him? I went to the back door and locked the cat flap before slipping outside, closing the door softly behind me. I stood listening in the dark, not knowing what I was expecting to hear but there was nothing, not even the usual comforting sounds from the stables as the horses were out.

A staccato sound cracked through the night. My mouth went dry as my breath caught. Forcing myself to breathe normally, I heard another burst of gunfire and ran back inside.

Carlton was in the kitchen. "Did I just hear what I thought I heard?"

I nodded dumbly. What we had feared was here. Where was Trent? I wanted to do something, but there was nothing I could do. I paced the kitchen, arms crossed over my chest, phone clamped in one hand, my eyes fixed on the quarry tiles as I followed a line of grouting up and down, up and down. Carlton kept a watch on the lane. I could hear Grace telling the children stories as she huddled with them, wrapped in blankets on the settee.

My phone vibrated, making me jump. Thank God, it was Trent. I hadn't realised how much I'd needed to hear his voice, to hear he was all right. I wanted to hear that everyone was okay, that it was all over, but his voice, low and authoritative, shocked me.

"Grayson, we're pinned down in what's looking like a diversion. One vehicle is heading in your direction. We believe target to be Grace and the children. I need you to get them out of there." I swallowed, something jagged in my throat as I wondered how he was expecting me to do that.

"How?" I managed.

"Take your pickup, get them off the estate. Carlton, can he..." A loud burst of gunfire coming out of the phone made me jump again. A grunting curse, silence. Nothing more. I stared at the phone in horror; my knees buckled beneath me as my heart felt as though it was collapsing in on itself. Carlton had heard the shots and spoke to me firmly, not letting me dwell on the horrific possibilities.

"He'll be fine, Grayson. What did he say?"

I couldn't make my voice work.

"Grayson," he barked fiercely, "what did he say?" An order this time. He gripped my chin, forcing me to look at him, forcing me to tear my gaze from the phone and my thoughts from Trent's fate.

"One vehicle headed this way, target Grace and the children. He – he told me to get them out of here. Use the pickup." I looked up at him, feeling desperate at my uselessness in this situation. We both froze, hearing a vehicle, still at a distance but approaching rapidly. Carlton dashed to the front window, peering out. He glanced back at me, his expression telling me all I needed to know. Get a grip, I told myself.

Using the pickup was not an option now; they'd be on us before we got out of the gate. A solution presented itself; not an easy one, but our enemies might not expect it. I collected a couple of bags from the boot room and calling Carlton into the kitchen whispered my plan, stuffing supplies into the bags as I did so. I needed him to give us as much cover as he could. I knew that, like Trent, Carlton carried a gun, but one gun would only give us limited time. Carlton nodded his agreement to the plan, and went to rouse Grace and the children as I grabbed a torch to shove into one of the bags.

At the back door I met the others, Grace pushing the sleepy children's feet into their boots as they pulled on their jackets. I knelt in front of them, not wanting to frighten them as I explained, as gently as possible, the adventure in front of us. I saw their eyes widen at what I was expecting, and as I met Grace's eyes I saw her resolve grow at what I needed her to do. Handing her one of the bags to carry, I swung the other on to my back.

78

We all heard the vehicle slowing down before it reached the cottage, squealing brakes being applied to a vehicle being driven too fast. I hustled everyone out the door. Carlton and I exchanged loaded glances as I bent to touch Susie's head then I slipped out, silently closing the door behind me.

Crossing the yard, we stayed in the shadow of the buildings until we got to the tack room. I unlocked it, and without turning on the light grabbed and passed round bridles, pulling a stirrup leather from a saddle to make do as a neck-strap for Monty. Urging everyone to move fast, I crept out to the paddock.

As we went I heard shouting and hoped Carlton was all right. He hadn't questioned my decision to leave him behind, I realised, and I felt ashamed at my selfishness. I hadn't questioned my decision either: it had seemed the only solution.

The horses, though bemused at this unusual night-time activity, let us catch them. Putting Regan's bridle on over the head collar he was already wearing, I led him to the gate, feeling his bewilderment at these goings-on in the dark. The others followed me through the gate as I grabbed the lead ropes from the fence and crammed them into my bag.

The moon was very nearly full, everyone's faces ashen in its cold light. Sophia and Reuben jumped on to their ponies as Grace manoeuvred Monty, already jittery, alongside the post and rail fence, using it for a leg-up. I saw her wrap her hand in his mane as she grabbed the neck-strap. Though she was a confident rider, I'd never seen her ride bareback before, and she'd need all the help she could get on a horse that was skittish at the best of times.

More shouting broke out. I thought I could hear Carlton's voice. Then a shocking spray of gunfire, accompanied by the sound of breaking glass. My heart jolted. Regan, startled by the noise, shot forward, but rather than hold him back I ran alongside, leaping up the stack of jumping blocks piled outside the arena and throwing myself on to his back. Regan kept going as we flew towards the barn, the others following.

More gunfire, single shots in response, further gunfire coming from the direction of the Manor as we rounded the back of the barn. I intended to leave the yard by taking an uphill route through the trees. Looking up briefly, I could see the Manor across the parkland in the distance, but it was too far away to see any detail.

Spotting the gap in the trees I was aiming for, I glanced back to check on the others. Grimly determined, Grace was hanging on tight. Then her mouth opened in alarm at something ahead, and as I turned forward again I saw a man move in front of us, coming out of the shadows, blocking our escape route. I hauled on the reins, slipping forward on Regan's back as I did so. Grace pulled Monty up alongside, and the children fell in behind.

The man was armed. If he hadn't been I'd have ridden straight through him, but he held the gun he trained on us two-handed. He appeared as surprised to have come across us escaping as we were to find him in our way. But having brought us to a halt, he didn't seem to know what to do next, and as we stared at each other I tried to think of a way out of the situation. Then, during a lull in the gunfire, he yelled. A warning? Or for help? I couldn't tell as I didn't understand a word of what he said, but I heard a car's engine roar into life as if roused by his words, and at that precise moment a shot rang out. Just one, that sounded like the crack of a whip. A spray of blood exploded from side of the man's head. He remained upright for the briefest moment, then crumpled to the ground as limp as a rag doll.

I froze, not believing what I'd seen. Bile rose in my throat. Grace, stronger than I, urged the children to look away, and sheltered them from the sight by blocking their view with Monty's body. I shook myself into action. The enemy vehicle was about to turn into the gateway, and before we could be caught in its headlights I hurried everyone along, leading the way around the body and into the trees. The path we were taking was overgrown and barely one horse wide. The ponies followed me, with Grace bringing up the rear as we all clambered up the steep incline. I felt myself slip on Regan's back, and wrapped my legs tighter around him, my fingers buried in his mane as I clung on, calling back for everyone to hold on tight.

I hoped, if I'd got my geography of the paths right, that once we'd scrambled through this tough uphill section we would eventually meet up with one of the more familiar paths. I thought there'd be more light on a wider path; at the moment it was difficult to see anything, the moonlight blocked out by foliage. Cursing under my breath as an unseen branch smacked across my forehead, I called a warning back to Grace, wishing I'd made time for us to have brought our hats. I let one hand go from Regan's mane and rubbed the stinging pain, then cursed again as my knee slammed into a tree. I allowed Regan to find his own way as I held on tight, and leant forward to help him stay in balance as he climbed.

Aware of shouts amid occasional shots, which I hoped meant Carlton was still in action, we rode up to the top of the incline, and I took a deep breath of relief once the path plateaued and opened out a little. Headlights pierced the woods to our left then disappeared again, leading me to believe the vehicle had turned around and would now be heading out of the yard and along the lane, hoping to find us further on.

I brought Regan to a halt as everyone reached the top of the hill and came to a standstill beside me. It had been hard work getting up this far; the horses were blowing and, like us, needed a minute's rest. I took advantage of that to check that everyone was okay, though I couldn't imagine any of us felt as if we'd ever be okay again. I received the mute bobbing of heads to my questions and settled for that.

Once the horses' breathing had slowed we set off again, still stumbling through the undergrowth and dodging around trees but at least it was flat, and a few minutes later we were relieved to come across one of the wider paths. We stopped again as I tried to get my bearings. It had been a while since I'd heard any engine noise, and our enemies seemed to have passed further on along the lane. There was no more gunfire – we could hear nothing but the silence around us. Perhaps it was all over – and if it was, who had won? Until we knew that, it wouldn't be safe for us to reveal ourselves, and for the time being we would press ahead with my plan.

We turned left along the path we were on, walking two abreast. The going was not so hard, but we were more vulnerable than before when we were struggling through the undergrowth, without so much tree cover it was lighter, which made it easier to see – or be seen, I thought anxiously. It was eerily quiet now. I kept listening for movement but there was none. Even the nocturnal animals were absent, no doubt disturbed by the activity and noise.

I realised we were about to hit the lane, which we needed to cross to get on to a similar path. All was still and noiseless as Regan stepped out on to the road. We were half way across when an explosion of light to our left robbed us of our night vision, accompanied by the roar of an engine bursting into life a hundred metres or so from us as a vehicle swerved out on to the road, accelerating fast. I heard Sophia squeal behind me as I yelled for everyone to follow, and we set off at full pelt straight across the road and back on to a familiar riding track. I shouted to Grace to take the lead as I pulled back a little, allowing all three of them to pass me then pulling Regan in behind.

I looked back, and could see for the first time the silhouette of the vehicle as it travelled along the road. It was some sort of off-road-type Jeep, and I was relieved to see it carry on past the end of our path, sticking to the road. The problem was that the trees here were more spread out. I could see the Jeep travelling along the road, and as long as I could see them, they could see us. Our path had started to veer away from the road, though, and I knew it would soon take us out of their sight. I hoped they were not too familiar with the layout of the estate, and I hoped they hadn't guessed where we were going as we needed to make the most of the fact that this route to the farm was shorter than going by road. Unless we could get ahead of them now, there would be no slipping off the estate secretly after all.

Fumbling to get my phone out of my pocket, I called Porter, willing him to answer as we rode towards the farm.

"Grayson?"

"Porter, get the gate open. We're coming through and we've got company."

"Roger." I had no idea what he meant by that, but he'd gone. I slipped my phone back into my pocket and urged everyone on as fast as possible. Grace was having to hold Monty back from full flight to allow everyone else a chance of staying close to him, and the children were keeping up manfully. I could feel the ache in my legs so I knew they must be getting tired, and I had no idea if they were going to make the distance. I could see the outline of the farm buildings ahead. Our path met the road where both entered the farmyard, and although I could hear the Jeep's engine I could see no sign of it. I felt a small surge of hope that we might yet make it as we shot out of the end of the path and Grace led the charge towards the gate.

Porter was there, the gate was opening and Monty had already disappeared through the widening gap as the Jeep burst into the farmyard behind us. Zodiac and Benjy passed through as shots rang out. Porter grunted, his legs buckling under him as he fell.

I was also through, off the estate, but we were far from being safe. As I looked back all I could see was Porter lying motionless, and my heart sank further with this latest loss. I hoped the others hadn't seen.

Distracted I hadn't even noticed we'd crossed the road and were travelling along the edge of a field. I knew there were a few of these to go through. I drew alongside Reuben and Sophia, leaning down to look at them, shouting across, "Are you okay to carry on?" Both glanced over, grim-faced but firmly nodding.

I could hear the Jeep behind us. I didn't bother looking back. What was the point? It was coming and there was nothing I could do about it. We were already doing all we could, and that was to keep running.

We were passing the forest of conifers, which looked eerie in the silvery moonlight, the ranks of firs creepy in a way the woods on the estate were not.

I knew the entrance to the beach was only round the corner now. The lights behind me wavered up and down, shadows appearing and disappearing with each movement as the Jeep bounced along the rutted track. I doubted the occupants had any idea where we were going but were just doggedly following their prey, expecting we would run out of energy before we got much further.

We fled down the slope and on to the beach. My hopes of finding safety here had been dashed and I had no plan B, no idea how to get us out of this. I'd imagined arriving at this point at a more leisurely pace, without this feeling of exhaustion spreading through my legs, my arms, my body. I'd imagined getting the family to safety, hiding out in the cave until the danger was over. But now, as I looked out to sea at the shimmering silver track of the moon as it crossed the water towards us, I realised I'd failed. All I'd done was lead us into a trap, and everyone's effort – everyone's sacrifice, as my thoughts returned to Carlton and Porter – had been for nothing.

The beach lit up as the headlights reached the top of the slope behind us. We were not far from the cliffs at the far end, and the lights dipped down as the Jeep travelled down the slope, then up again as it levelled out on the sand. A couple of shots were fired, and I couldn't help thinking we were too far away for them to be accurate. But then Regan jolted under me, and I felt a stinging pain across my thigh. Swerving to one side, I zig-zagged Regan back and forth, snaking behind the children, hoping to make the target harder to hit. Then with some relief I realised we'd made it to the cliffs.

Monty baulked at the water, stopping short as it swirled menacing and black at his feet. Grace managed to stay on, her hands knotted in his mane, still clamped to the neck-strap. One look at her told me she'd had it. She'd had the hardest ride of any of us, and now her shoulders were hunched, her energy spent. Zodiac and Benjy plunged in, oblivious to the danger that Monty perceived. As I passed him I wrapped my legs tighter around Regan and leaned over to grab a handful of rein and head collar, hoping any further resistance from Monty wouldn't rip me from Regan's back. As our momentum carried us into the water I held tight to Monty's head collar, feeling the strain as the muscles through my arm and across my back screamed with the effort, then a sudden release as Monty shifted and followed us in, the fear of being left behind greater than the scary cold blackness around his legs. Pulling him along, we quickly got out to the point of the rocks, turned and rushed back towards the smaller beach to join the children; all of us, horses and humans, breathing heavily, sweating and shaking with exertion.

# Chapter 7

I slid from Regan's back. It felt a long way down into sand that gave way, throwing me off balance. I forced strength back into my trembling legs as I struggled to save myself from falling. Knowing we had to keep moving as far and as fast as we could in the trap I'd led us into, I looked over at the children and spoke softly.

"Okay, guys, time to get off." Both of them reacted immediately, sliding off, finding it easier than I had. Young bodies, I thought as I glanced anxiously at their mother. No movement.

Handing Regan's reins to Sophia, I came up to Monty and Grace. Running my hand first along his steaming neck, I then placed one hand on her knee, squeezing and gently shaking it, my other hand on hers that still tightly gripped mane and neck-strap as I looked up at her.

"Grace? Grace...look at me. We need to get under cover, you must get off now."

Her head moved slightly as her eyes met mine. I could see her fear.

"The children, Grace, we need to keep them safe," I urged, knowing this was what she would care about; this was what would get her moving. I used both my hands now to try to loosen hers, and as I did so she came to her senses. Her hands relaxed from their frozen position, and as she let go I braced myself to help steady her as she stumbled on landing. She breathed out in relief as she righted herself, indicating with a nod to me that she was all right.

Taking Regan's reins again, I led us up the beach. On getting to the entrance of the cave I knew how dark it would be in there so I stopped, took the bag off my back and pulled out the four lead ropes, throwing one to each of the others.

"Take the bridles off," I said, and soon we were leading each of the horses into the cave. There wasn't much light, but enough to allow me to find the tethering post Trent and I had installed the previous year. I tied up the horses, who were sweating, breathing heavily and exhausted, and, patting each one, I thanked them silently for their efforts. Finally I passed my hand over Regan's flank. It was wet and sticky, and my hand was dark with blood as I held it in the moonlight. I took a minute to examine the wound on my leg. The adrenaline pumping through me was overriding any pain, and although there was a blood-soaked patch on my ripped jodhpurs only a small amount of blood was oozing from what appeared to be a flesh wound.

Turning to the others, who had collapsed in a heap by the cave opening, I went back outside, gathered up the bridles and dumped them in a pile inside the cave. As I did so I noticed our clear trail up the beach.

We had no idea who was in the Jeep or how many of them they were, but they had been determined in following us to this point, and I didn't see any reason why they would stop now. I could already imagine them wading into the water as they followed the rocks, and us, out to sea. All we could do was put off the inevitable for as long as possible. From the sea the entrance to the cave was hidden. With a bit of luck they might think we had ridden on to the next bay. Bending down, I picked up a pile of debris that had been washed up, mostly seaweed but it also included a piece of tattered sack-like material attached to a short length of frayed rope. Going down to where the waves had stopped washing away our tracks, I retraced my steps backwards up the beach, rubbing my bundle of flotsam over the sand, obliterating our tracks as best as I could.

All I could think about was that I needed to buy us as much time as I could before help arrived. I couldn't think about the fact that help might not arrive. I couldn't think about that at all. Finishing my task, I backed into the cave, then threw the debris back out on to the beach.

I crouched in front of the others where they were huddled together and I had to stir them into action.

"Come on, we have to keep moving. If they follow us..." And of course they will, I thought. "We have to make it as hard for them as we can."

Though there was exhaustion in the faces staring back at me, I dragged everyone to their feet. Taking a torch out of my bag, I picked our way to the back of the cave, trying to avoid the small rocks that poked up out of the sand, waiting to stub our toes and trip us up. I flicked on the light as soon as we walked into the shadows. From my brief explorations the previous summer I knew the cave went back a long way, and I hoped if our hunters weren't prepared, if they hadn't brought torches and if we hid as far back as possible they might not be able to find us. It was a lot of ifs.

I looked at the horses regretfully as we passed, feeling terrible at leaving them in this condition. I'd not been able to offer them any water, they had no hay to occupy them, and having been left sweating from the strenuous exercise on this muggy summer's night, they'd now been left in a cool, damp cave and were going to get chilled. Same would apply to us, I thought. I could already feel the sweat cooling on my skin. At least Carlton knew where we were going, I reassured myself. He would come as soon as he could...as soon as he could, I repeated slowly. What if he couldn't? What if he was... I forced myself to confront this fear. What if he was dead? Then no one would know where we were. No, I corrected myself, Porter knew we'd gone out of the gate. That would be enough to give others a good idea as to where we were heading. Porter – as the vision of his still body came back to me I realised with increasing despair that no one had any idea where we were. Desperate to let someone know I pulled my phone out of my pocket. No signal, unsurprisingly. It was too late – I had well and truly messed up.

At the back of the cave we no longer had sand beneath our feet, but rock: uneven slabs interspersed with jagged edges, making our progress slow. We held each other's hands in a chain formation to help steady and guide one another. Sophia's hand felt small and cold in mine as I held it tightly. I thought we'd probably reached about as far back as I'd been before. Last time I'd turned back from the claustrophobic dark and damp, wanting to return to the sun, but now the darkness was all-consuming whichever way we turned.

A voice called out in the dark behind us, echoing in the cavernous space. I jumped, flicked off the torch and stopped still. "Hush!" I whispered to the others as I listened for more, trying to quieten my breathing which to my ears sounded loud enough to be echoing back at the intruder. A man's voice came again. I didn't understand what was being said. A foreign language, and therefore clearly not the help I was hoping for. A second voice answered, deeper and gruffer than the first. Then there was silence. They were either leaving or creeping up on us. I saw no torchlight from their direction, which was a good sign. Perhaps they were ill-equipped for following us. I pulled gently on Sophia's hand and we stumbled on. I risked turning on the torch, thinking we were far enough back now for it not to be seen. The sound of us shuffling around in the dark as we tried to find our footing without light might be more of a draw.

The cave had narrowed considerably, the roof now lower. Our escape route seemed to be petering out, but I stuck to my original resolution to make it as difficult as possible for our potential captors. As I pushed on I wondered how long it would take for them to find us; how much time it would take for them to drag us back out on to the beach. I allowed myself a brief moment to imagine their dismay if, on doing so, they found Trent and the others waiting for them. A good ending, I thought, but right now about as likely as a fairy-tale.

Too busy escaping, too busy trying to hang on to Regan, I'd pushed Trent from my mind when Carlton had snapped me out of the horror at hearing the shots, Trent's grunt, the silence of the deadened phone. Carlton's "He'll be fine" had been so definite, but how could he be? Wanting to get me moving, he'd said what I'd needed to hear, verbally kicking me back into action. I knew Trent could be dead, my worst fear realised, a sob caught in my throat, though I would not allow the tears to come. It'd be no good if I fell apart now, I told myself fiercely, and I tried to convince myself maybe he hadn't been hit, maybe he'd dived for cover, maybe we'd been cut off. It was a lot of maybes.

Trying to clear my mind of these muddled thoughts, I told myself to concentrate on our current predicament. No good dreaming about being rescued, I had to focus on the here and now. Coming out of my reverie, I noticed we'd not yet reached a dead end. I cast the torch around. Rock encased us, and while we could only walk in single file, the cave had not diminished in size. It was damp and there was still a salty tang in the air, though it was not as clean and fresh as it had been in the main cave.

My thoughts were interrupted by a sob from behind me. I turned quickly to see Sophia bravely trying to wipe away her tears on the collar of her jacket. I caught Grace's look of concern as she reached for Sophia, hugging her tightly. Reuben quietly moved closer to me, subdued with exhaustion. I'd pushed them all too far. We needed a break.

I sank gratefully to the ground, my legs collapsing under me, and the others did the same. I whispered to Grace to pass me her bag, then took out a bottle of water, only then acknowledging how thirsty I was. I handed it around and everyone gulped greedily. There wasn't much left when we'd all had our fill. I managed to stop myself finishing it and put it back in the bag, then pulled out bars of chocolate. It was a small thing, but good to see everyone's eyes light up. Sophia's tears had stopped and she was being cuddled by her mother, so I checked on Reuben.

"Are you okay?" He nodded, and I tried again. "Are you cold?"

"No," he mumbled as he shivered, and I rubbed my hands up and down his arms briskly, hoping to impart at least a little warmth.

Then, knowing I was going to have to move things along, I turned to Grace. "Have you heard anything?"

"Not really," she replied. "I thought a couple of times I could hear voices, but then heard nothing else so decided they were only in my imagination." I'd heard and thought the same. It could be our anxious minds playing games on us, or the enemy could be keeping as quiet as we were and creeping closer every moment.

This thought spurred me on as I was also aware of the cold seeping into me, and at least when moving we were keeping warm...ish.

We clambered to our feet and carried on walking. The break had done us good. I felt better able to concentrate on the challenge facing us now, rather than only being able to deal with the task of putting one foot in front of the other. It only now dawned on me that we were actually in a passage and not just disappearing into the far reaches of the cave. When Trent and I had come to the beach he'd told me of the tales that surrounded this part of the coast: smugglers' caves and tunnels back up to the village for the goods to be taken along. Although the cave part had been believable – we were in the cave after all – the tunnel bit had seemed unlikely, and I'd assumed it was an exaggerated piece of local folklore. It appeared I was wrong. Unless I was mistaken, it felt as though the passage we were in was on an incline.

I jumped, definitely hearing a noise. I could see Grace had been startled too. I was pleased to see she looked stronger, with a spark in her eye as she urged the children on. Eager to make the most of this new burst of energy, I turned and smacked straight into a jagged piece of overhanging rock. I cried out at the sudden pain, my hand coming up to my face, my icy skin feeling good on the wound as my head swam for a moment. I bent double, leaning against the damp wall as I tried to collect myself, blinking away the tears that had come with the shock. Grace moved closer, concerned, but I waved her away. Damn it, I thought, I'd tried to keep silent, but if we'd been able to hear them, they must certainly have heard me cry out. I'd split my eyebrow open. I could feel it sticky wet on my fingers, could see the blood in the torchlight. It didn't seem too bad, only a bit messy, I thought as I gathered myself and motioned for us to go on. I didn't want our pursuers catching up. I could feel wetness trickling down my face, though I tried to leave the wound alone, knowing it would soon dry up and stop bleeding. But I wished I had some painkillers for the thumping ache that now radiated out from my eyebrow.

The passage was changing, rock being replaced by dark earth, but more telling were the signs of human activity. Beams and struts now shored up the walls and the tunnel roof, and this I found alarming. When I'd investigated the cave the previous summer, claustrophobia had put me off going any further and I'd returned to the sunlight. On entering the cave this evening I'd been driven by fear and adrenaline to go on as far as possible, never believing anything like this lay ahead. The darkness in itself had been claustrophobic, but I'd refused to allow that fear to take over.

Now it was a different story. The passage needed to be held up. From the groove marks on the walls, parts, if not all, had been dug out, manmade, and suddenly all I could think about was the weight of earth above us. My breath stuck in my throat as the air changed. No sea tang now, but a smell of earth. Usually it was one of my favourite scents, rain on moisture-deprived woodland, redolent of beautiful rich soil coming up at me as I rode through the trees, making up for the fact that I'd been soaked through by an unexpected shower. Here though the air felt stale, and I suddenly wondered if there would be enough of it to go around, what with all of us breathing heavily as we were with the route march speed I was setting. I could almost feel the air running out, my breaths becoming shallower, panic sweeping over me as I imagined what suffocation would be like.

I tried to shake off these thoughts, but having anticipated that at any moment it was likely we would find the tunnel had caved in and we would have to turn around and face our fate, my mind now jumped to the likelihood of the roof collapsing on us. It must be unstable, I thought. It would have been many years since anyone had come down here; the walls were probably crumbling, the props and struts rotten. I could see the whole lot crashing down, burying us, and I didn't think it would be like being crushed under rocks, which we wouldn't know much about. It would be a painfully slow way to die, and no one knew we were here. As my panic built I could feel myself starting to shake. I drove on at a relentless pace, not allowing the others to slacken speed in my need to escape the darkness.

For God's sake, get a grip, I told myself. Now was not the time to end up as some pathetic shaking wreck, unable to go on because of a bit of claustrophobia. There were worse things in life to have to deal with. I knew that only too well, and I needed to fight these overwhelming feelings. Others were counting on me to get them out of this, and it would not help if I went to pieces. I tried to reassure myself that at any moment we were likely to come to the end of the tunnel. I was assuming it would be up in the village somewhere, and then we could seek help and this would all be over.

Forcing myself to take deep breaths to calm down, I turned my thoughts to lighter things. Imagining I was riding Regan through the woods in a sunny bright shower; imagining the earthy smell rising up from the woodland floor imagining fresh air and sunshine and warmth. Warmth.

Though I was sweating with exertion, my sweat was cooling too quickly so I felt clammy and shivering, and I knew the warmth I needed. Trent. I imagined him wrapping himself around me as we lay in a tangle of bed sheets. I imagined the warmth that came with being loved by him, from knowing he was there. Strong, dependable and warm. I gulped as my thoughts dived to another dark place. What if he was gone? What if I was alone again? It kept happening: I kept losing people. My parents – although my memories of them were nonexistent, I remembered the feeling of loss, the loneliness growing up. Eva, my treasured daughter, whose death I would never recover from. If I'd now lost Trent, I didn't know what would become of me.

I thought back to that moment only a few weeks ago when I'd nearly left the estate, afraid of the very thing that could now have happened. I forced myself away from these black thoughts. I couldn't afford to let despair set in. Turning instead to more practical matters, hoping they would stabilise my emotions, I wondered how long we'd been walking and briefly shone the light on my watch. It was just after 2am. No wonder we were all flagging. I hadn't looked at my watch before so I didn't know how long we'd been going, but at a guess I thought we'd probably left the stables at around eleven. My thoughts briefly distracted me again as I worried about the horses, wondering if they were all right. Then back to the task in hand. I reckoned it could have taken as long as one to one and a half hours to get to the beach. It had taken quite a while to get through the woods, so that meant we had probably been walking for an hour to an hour and a half. I thought people walked at about four miles an hour, so we could be as much as six miles along this tunnel by now. No – even though I'd been moving us along as fast as possible, we were considerably slower than that, lucky if we were making half that speed. So, two to three miles, still quite a distance. I certainly wouldn't have wanted to be a smuggler carrying goods up this passage. As my thoughts turned to wondering what they might have been smuggling, I realised how tired I was. My head dull and woolly, aching from the crack it had received, and with my difficulty in concentrating and my thoughts all over the place, I wondered if I was becoming a little delirious.

Suddenly I felt Reuben pulling on the back of my jacket as he said, "I know where we are."

In my dazed state I wondered how that could be possible, but when I looked around I could see the passage had changed. It was now solidly built in dark red-brown brick. I stopped walking, and with huge relief collapsed to the floor. The others sat down too, and we huddled together in our exhaustion as Grace passed round our remaining bottle of water and handed out handfuls of the biscuits I'd packed. I asked Reuben how he knew where we were.

"I found this place – well, it looks like this place – when I was exploring last summer."

Grace's eyebrows rose, but all she said was "Where does it lead to?"

Reuben paused for a moment, trying to swallow his biscuit, and took a swig of water. "It comes out…"

I put my finger to my lips. "Not so loud."

"It comes out in the shed at the end of the vegetable garden," he whispered.

"I know where he means," said Grace, 'it's an old brick building. We call it the shed. It's where the gardeners store lots of their stuff. How did you come across it?" she asked. I could imagine she couldn't quite believe how far Reuben's explorations had taken him.

"I like finding secret places on the estate, and the building was open one day and I looked inside before the gardeners shooed me away. I'd seen some doors in there that looked like a cupboard, although they were on a slope up from the floor." He showed what he meant by gesticulating with his hand, and I imagined they must have been like the doors at the back of pubs for the barrels to be delivered through. "…And I wanted to see what was inside the cupboard so I went back when the garden was empty…" He tailed off as he realised he was on the brink of telling us something he shouldn't have done. I saw him look up at his mother through his long eyelashes; a look that would be hard to resist.

"Go on," she prompted him gently, "you've got this far."

He sighed. "Well, I went back and it was all locked up, so I…" He looked down guiltily before confessing, "So I went round the back. There's a small space between the wall and the building, so I went along there and broke a window." I heard the intake of breath from Grace, but she didn't say anything. Reuben added in a rush, "It wasn't like I broke the glass, but the window was really old and loose, and when I pulled at it the catch didn't hold, so I broke that off and climbed in." I was quite impressed by

96

his adventurous spirit but, mindful of Grace's feelings, I tried not to look too admiringly at him.

"So what did you do then?" I asked, needing to move the story along. I was very aware that our potential captors could be drawing ever closer, even though we hadn't heard anything for a while.

"I opened up the big doors that were in the corner. It didn't look like anyone had opened them for a long time, but when I did I could see right down in this tunnel. At least, like I said, I think it was this tunnel...it was built like this." And he ran his hand over the brickwork of the wall. "I went down it a little way, but it was a bit scary even though I had my torch, so I turned back." He ended with a shrug as if it was nothing out of the ordinary. Goodness only knew what else he'd found on his explorations.

"Okay, thanks, Reuben, we'd better get moving again," I said, trying not to groan when my body complained as I pushed myself up off the ground.

I cast the torch back down the passage, running it over the earthen walls and the tunnel roof, briefly examining the wooden beams of the framework. I wondered if I should attempt to cause a cave-in behind us to slow down and perhaps even stop those we suspected were coming up the tunnel. I tested one of the upright posts with my weight. Feeling it give a little, creaking as it moved against the board above, a light shower of dirt falling, I felt fluttering panic rise up in me again at the thought of following through with my theory. In practice it might bring down more than I was expecting, and would I be able to get out of the way quick enough? On the other hand, there was no guarantee I'd bring down enough to block the tunnel sufficiently, and what if we found we couldn't get out of the doors at the end, supposing this even was the same tunnel? What if the doors had been locked since Reuben had been exploring? There were too many unanswered questions that might mean we'd be trapped in here with no way out, no phone signal, and – as was likely, and I had to face it again – the very real possibility that no one knew we were here. That thought depressed me enough to decide against my destructive plan.

I took the lead again as we started up the passage, though now I was a little more hopeful. We hadn't been caught yet, and it felt like we were coming to the end. How far would anyone have been able to build in brick anyway? It couldn't be that far, I reasoned, and it was a lot safer being surrounded by solid walls. It definitely felt as if we were in a better situation than we'd been in for a while.

Barely a minute later my torch shone on a brick wall directly ahead of us. My heart sank, thinking the passage had been blocked off, but then I realised with relief that this literally was the end. Raising my torch, I could see the doors above us, lower where they met the brick wall, then they slanted upwards into the tunnel roof. We stopped, allowing ourselves a brief celebration which consisted of us grinning at each other; a moment's respite. I was the tallest and the only one with any chance of reaching the doors. Even then I could only just manage to place my palms on their surface with my arms nearly at full stretch. This could be a problem. After warning the others what I was about to do, I turned off the torch and plunged us into darkness.

"Reuben," I whispered, "when you opened these doors, did they make a noise?"

"Yeah, they made a terrible racket."

Brilliant.

I reached up and placed my hands on one half of the door, the wood rough on my skin as I tried to push it up. I mentally crossed my fingers, hoping that I'd be able to shift it at least a little; at least enough to prove it wasn't locked. It was heavy, good solid wood, but as I pushed I felt it give. It rose a couple of inches, and I lowered it gently.

It wasn't locked, but now, having tested it, I didn't know if I was going to be able to lift it as far as I would need to. I didn't have enough strength for more than one attempt, and knew I was just going to have to go for it. There was nothing I could do about the noise. My overriding desire was to get out of what increasingly felt like a prison. I desperately craved fresh air again, so planting my hands back on the door I silently counted to three then drove up hard and fast, pushing up and over to the side as I struggled against the weight. The door groaned, unused hinges screeching as the old wood creaked. I stretched as far as I could, my fingertips the only things left in contact. The load lightened as the door reached the point of no return and fell back under its own weight – open.

From where we stood, the crash of the door slamming back was deafening. As I collapsed back, gasping with the effort, I imagined that sound echoing across the estate, drawing our enemies towards us.

Dust and debris, shaken into life by the reverberations of the falling door, rained down on us, and, as I waved my hand in front of my face to clear the air, I looked up, pleased to see the edges of the hole framing the lighter room above. Reuben had said the building had windows, and though it was still night, the darkness of a summer's night was nothing compared to the blackness of the tunnel.

The next challenge was going to be getting out. The bottom edge of the door was buried in a wooden frame which was a little above my head height. I glanced round at the others, pleased I could now pick them out in the dark.

"Grace, can you give me a leg up?"

She nodded, moving towards me, cupping her hands by her knees as she braced herself, her back against the wall. I put my foot in her hands and counted down, then launched myself upwards, flopping up and out of the door much like a sea lion coming out of a pool, though considerably less gracefully. The edge of the wooden frame bit into my hips as I wiggled forward. I planted my hands to each side as I struggled to hoist myself out of the hole, my legs flailing behind. One last heave and I rolled over onto my back, giving myself a moment as I lay there, gratefully taking in a deep breath of fresh...ish air – we were, after all, still in a shed.

Eventually I sat up, crawled back over to the hole, and reached down to grasp Reuben's outstretched hand. I pulled him up at the same time as Grace pushed from below, depositing him next to me before returning for Sophia. Lastly came Grace, needing two hands and more effort.

Looking at Reuben's small size, I said, "How did you get out when you came exploring?"

"I used that ladder, over by the door."

A shame he hadn't mentioned that before.

I took a moment to look around. It was still dark, but not the absolute absence of light we'd experienced in the tunnel. Cobwebby wire-meshed windows on each side of the shed door as well as smaller windows on the back wall allowed moonlight in, giving enough light to see by. I closed the door to the tunnel, wincing at the noise that came from the hinges, then, looking around, spotted some bags of compost leaning up against the far wall. I carried one over and dropped it on the tunnel doors. Grace and the children followed my lead, Grace dragging the bags across the floor while the children carried them over between them, until eventually enough bags weighed down the doors and I was confident that no one would be able to shift the doors from below and follow us out.

For the first time in what felt like an age I breathed out a sigh of relief, and we sat in a small circle on the floor, exhausted and filthy, as we finished the small amount of water we had left and handed out the last of the biscuits.

I looked at the tired faces around me and I wondered how much more they had left in them. I was impressed by the bravery and strength Sophia and Reuben had shown; clearly they took after their parents. Not an ounce of whinging or moaning had come from either of them, but as both now leaned against their mother they didn't look that far from sleep.

We were now in the early hours of the morning, and as I contemplated our next move I realised I could hear nothing. Well, nothing other than the munching of biscuits. No gunfire; absolute silence. I went over to the door and tried the handle. It was, as I'd expected, locked or bolted, or both. Peering round the edge of a window that was dirty and thick with dust I struggled to see anything, though I was reluctant to wipe away the dirt in case someone was looking. I told myself I was being paranoid. Why would anyone be watching an old building in the corner of the vegetable garden? As my eyes adjusted I found I could pick out the shapes of the garden in the moonlight. The Manor was further away, but comfortingly there were a few lights shining from windows: a welcome sight.

I went back to the others and pulled out my phone. There were a number of missed calls – none from Trent. Now, I thought as I called him, the moment of truth. There was no response at all: no ringing, no opportunity to leave a voicemail, nothing. It was as if the phone was...I couldn't say it. I couldn't think it. I tried a couple of others – Cavendish, Carlton – both times straight to voicemail. At least that was better than nothing. I left a message on each phone about our situation, but wondered why they didn't answer. I didn't make too much of it to spare the others, but saw the look that came over Grace's face and had to turn away.

I gently brought my fingers up to my eyebrow, tentatively feeling the wound. Though it was tender to the touch, the bleeding had stopped. I could feel the crusty scab and left that alone. I tried to rub away the dried blood that, by the tight, dry feel of my skin, had streaked down my face. I examined the wound on my leg. Dry now and bruised. I'd been lucky the bullet hadn't gone deeper. I thought back to Regan and hoped his wound was similarly shallow.

Looking back over at the doors that led to the tunnel, I couldn't help but think for a moment about Cavendish's ancestors and wonder if they could have had anything to do with the smuggling. Grace interrupted my thoughts.

"I had heard they were a colourful bunch." She smiled over at me. Great minds think alike. I grinned back.

I stared up at the moonlit window as I muttered, "What should we do?"

I was out of answers, my brain not functioning as it should, and I wanted all the help I could get. I wanted the cavalry to put in an appearance; I wanted knights in shining armour to come crashing through the door.

"I think we should leave here. I think we should try to get to the house while we have the darkness on our side," Grace whispered. "We can get across the garden in the shadows, creep through one of the rear doors, hide out somewhere until we can work out what's gone on..." She tailed off.

I hated to dampen her enthusiasm but I thought we might be better off staying where we were. I thought we were well hidden, and by the morning we might be able to tell if it was safe to come out or not, and if it wasn't we were less likely to be found here than in the house. I thought the fact that we couldn't get hold of anyone spoke volumes. However, I could understand Grace's desire to get back to her home. She probably couldn't think of it in any way other than being her safe, comfortable home, not believing for a moment that anything bad could happen there.

Suddenly a thought clicked into place. I should have thought of it before, of course, but I could at least put it down to the stressful situation, exhaustion, fear, dehydration and the biscuit diet that was messing with my insides. I should call Sharpe. She was likely to be in the office, with a good phone signal, in charge of logistics and the hub of all things. She would know...

As I reached for my phone, Reuben grabbed my arm and shook it as he pointed to the front window, his finger jabbing the air to get my attention. "A shadow..." he whispered. Then we heard the bolt being tried on the door, the door moving ever so slightly at the pressure being put on it as the bolt, stiff with age, refused to budge easily as if putting up a last line of defence for us.

Someone had heard the noise we'd made escaping from the tunnel, and that someone had come to get us. I didn't think for one moment this was the cavalry or a knight in shining armour. Their entrance would have been upfront, heroic and, I'd like to have thought, gilded with a touch of flamboyance.

This approach was stealthy, and I felt the hairs on the back of my neck rise. Grace and I pushed the children behind us, Sophia whimpering in fear, as we faced the door. The bolt suddenly shot free and hit home. Then the handle started to turn, oh...so...slowly. Grace grabbed my arm and whispered, "What shall we do?" I shrugged, raising my hands, palms uppermost, to show her I was out of ideas. Giving ourselves up had to be the only option.

# Chapter 8

The door creaked open but no one appeared. I feared the sound of my heart beating might drown out any words, so loudly was my blood pulsing through my ears. The silence stretched out, building the tension like the interminable wait when a winner's name is about to be revealed in a competition, everyone straining for the result.

When it came, the voice was male, heavily accented, the words spoken softly, but with an edge to them that couldn't be ignored. "Come out."

No "with your hands in the air" or any extraneous words. It was as if he didn't anticipate us coming at him brandishing weapons. Either that or he was very confident. From the sound of it he knew who he was dealing with, and although his voice was surprisingly gentle he made me believe he was a man who was not going to brook any nonsense. I gulped, suddenly finding it hard to swallow.

"Do not make me come in and get you."

No second request, just a threat spoken in the same calm tone as if he expected obedience without the need to raise his voice.

I thought quickly. We had no choices left open. We needed to keep alive until the others could reach us. They would eventually pick up our messages and know where we were, though I could've kicked myself that I hadn't thought about Sharpe until it was too late. I'd messed up again.

I nodded at Grace and we walked hesitantly towards the door. I went first, putting my hand out to push it open still further. As I stepped outside I felt a blade at my throat. I involuntarily stretched my chin up, and though a natural reaction it was a bad one as it bared by neck more openly to his knife. A hand whipped across my mouth, stifling any sound I might be tempted to make. He snatched my body to his, holding me tight against him. A rank sour smell of body odour wafted up at me. His or mine? I didn't know. His skin was dry and rough on my face, with a burnt metallic tang laced with a background of grease. As he positioned me between him and the Manor I thought for one moment of those on duty on the roof, wondering if they were still there. He must have thought so to position me like this. My captor forced me forward, his knees banging into the back of mine, and I realised a second man had slipped out of the shadows and moved in behind us.

A harsh whisper close to my ear. "If you will stay silent I'll remove my hand."

I nodded quickly, glad to get rid of his filthy hand, my eyes searching for my first sight of him.

"Keep your head still."

I did. His hand moved down on to my right shoulder, his arm across my chest holding me closer than ever, the other keeping the knife at my throat. I thought through my self-defence moves, working out which to use, then realised it was futile to try anything while the others could be at risk. Best to keep my powder dry.

I heard Grace give a small yelp behind me, then the door closed. The man who was holding me said, "Sophia and Reuben, you are to come with us. Do nothing to raise the alarm or we will hurt your mother – very badly."

Silence. I imagined their frightened little faces staring back at him, nodding their capitulation. Interesting that he knew their names. It stood to reason he also already knew which one of us was Grace. He forced me back into the shadow of the wall as we made our way towards the Manor.

I hadn't been in the vegetable garden before, but knew it was a little way behind the Manor near the kitchen door. I tried to get my bearings. Glancing up I scoured the roofline for any sign of life, finding none as we passed behind the Manor, and I knew we would soon come out into the courtyard. My back ached because of the angle I was being made to walk at, and I wondered about their plan. They couldn't have known where we were. If they had known that we'd disappeared into the tunnel, either because they'd been the ones following us or because someone else had reported back, they wouldn't have known any more than we did about where it was going to come out. So they must have come upon us purely by chance. No doubt the sound of the door falling had alerted them. They'd been lucky so far, but would that continue? Did they have a vehicle nearby for their escape? Were they the only ones left, or were there others that even now were coming to join them? I didn't fancy our chances at getting away from the two of them, let alone any more. Although from the way we were moving, quietly and keeping to the shadows, it didn't seem as if they were in control of the estate, which was a good sign.

Pausing at the courtyard entrance, I was turned and kept in the shadows as we made our way round until we stopped in front of a door. I'd never been through it, but knew we were at the Forsters' cottage. The arm disappeared from around me as my captor pulled my hands behind my back, and I felt him wrap something round my wrists before they were tightly brought together by a narrow strip with sharp edges which bit into my skin immediately. It'd happened so quickly I was taken by surprise and inhaled sharply at the discomfort. I gathered Grace was getting the same treatment behind me because I heard the voice say, "Do not run or I will catch you, and you will regret it." And he didn't have to expand on how unpleasant that would be.

He moved in front of me and I saw him, the back of him, for the first time. A little taller than me, his hair dark and closely cropped, shoulders broad under black well-fitted clothes. I could tell his body was like Trent's: ready for combat. One blow with his shoulder and the door burst inwards. He grabbed my arm, his fingers digging in, and I was hauled through it, the others following.

As I glanced back I saw the door pushed to by the other man, who dragged a small but heavy-looking chest across the hall, jamming it up against the door to keep it closed. The first man went through a doorway, and I followed him into a sitting room where he had drawn the curtains before putting on a side light. Worryingly, he didn't seem concerned about drawing attention to the fact that someone was here, and we had all followed him into the room before he turned to face us.

If it is true that we get the face we deserve as we age then he had already been a very bad man. His features in themselves were fine, with well-structured high cheekbones, his eyes narrow and very dark, almost black. His aquiline nose added arrogance to his gaze as he stared at me. I would have considered him good-looking, but everything about this face spoke of cruelty. The coldness in his eyes made them appear dead, like a shark's; his thin lips were twisted in a constant sneer, and as he turned his head in the light to look at Grace I saw the scar. It ran from high on his cheekbone down to the corner of his mouth where it puckered the skin, giving his lips that cruel twist.

I knew who this was, and a shiver of dread ran through me. This was Orlov, and I knew who he was because Trent had told us all at a briefing, and I knew about the scar because Trent was the one responsible for it, and Orlov did not look to me to be a forgiving sort.

He jerked his chin towards me, and asked, "Who are you?"

Grace swayed forward a little as she blurted out, "Sarah, her name is Sarah. She's no one, she's our groom. You could let her go."

I appreciated her bravery, but I wasn't going anywhere without the others. It seemed as if Orlov shared my view as he stared at me, unconvinced. Without replying, he indicated with his head for the other man to join him and they stood close, murmuring to each other in an unknown language, glancing over at us occasionally. I took the opportunity to check on the others. Like me, Grace had her hands bound behind her back with a cable tie, but I was pleased to see the children didn't. Not completely heartless then, I thought.

The other man was ugly, there was no kinder way to put it. The way his jaw jutted out suggested an underbite. His nose, broken many times by the look of it, was knobbly and crooked, his piggy eyes too close together and his sticking-out ears were comically large. It was an unfortunate face, and I had no idea who he was. What was clear, however, was which of the two was in charge.

They'd finished talking and Orlov nodded at Ugly, who withdrew a handgun from under his arm, moved towards Grace and, with the merest inclination of his head, drew her and the children a little away from me. I could see the children's scared little faces now and willed them to stay strong. I hoped, as much for me as for them, that they weren't about to be subjected to some unpleasant viewing.

I lifted my chin as I met Orlov's eyes, trying to hold back the look of defiance I wanted to throw at him. Keen to make myself feel strong while appearing meek was, I thought, the way to go. I hoped he would lose interest. As he moved closer I felt pinpricks of sweat break out on my skin at the menace that emanated from him. I forced myself to look down subserviently as he stopped in front of me.

"I don't think your name is Sarah...is it?"

I assumed it to be a rhetorical question and remained silent as he continued, "Let's find out who you are...shall we?" Reaching into my jacket he retrieved my phone, his hand brushing my breast quite deliberately. It made my skin crawl. Do not react, do not react, I repeated silently to myself, keeping my gaze downcast.

"Let's see. Who shall we call? Ah, Trent I think." His tongue rolled on the 'r' as he said the name. There was no change, no response from Trent's phone at all. Orlov looked at me steadily as if he knew this already. "Oh dear," he said, but it didn't sound like he was sorry, not one little bit. Do not react, do not react, I repeated as I wondered if he was responsible for what had happened to Trent, but he was immediately calling another number, and on loudspeaker we could all hear the ringing tone. I prayed it would go to voicemail.

"Grayson" came the urgent, cultured tone of Cavendish, and I heard Grace's relief in her exhaled breath and Sophia's quiet sob. "Just picked up your message, and was about to call. Grayson? Are you there?"

"Yes, she is here, Cavendish...with me, in a charming little house at the Manor," Orlov replied. "As are your wife and children. All perfectly safe...for the moment."

I could hear the strain in Cavendish's voice as he said, "I want to speak to my family."

Orlov shrugged, then held the phone out towards the group. Sophia was sobbing too hard now to get any words out, but Reuben's small voice said, "Daddy, come and get us."

"It's okay, Reuben, I'm coming. Look after your sister and Mum." Cavendish made his voice sound strong and comforting. "Grace?"

"I'm here, Henry, we're fine...really," Grace said shakily.

"Do not hurt them." His words carried their own threat.

"That will depend on you," Orlov said. 'Are you alone?"

"No."

"Put him on."

"Orlov." It was Trent's voice. Relief flooded through me; bubbles of joy burst deep within. Do not react, do not react, but I could feel renewed determination and resolve rising up in me on hearing his voice. I'd not let them get away with this. I'd not let them kidnap Grace and the children, if that was their plan.

"Who is Grayson, Trent?"

"She's the groom, of no consequence, you might as well let her go," Trent replied, sounding dismissive and, I thought, naively optimistic. Bizarrely, given the trying circumstances we were in, I felt slightly hurt at being of "no consequence".

Orlov's arm lashed out. His knife-blade sliced through my clothes and into the flesh of my upper arm. My scream of pain brought a hiss of fury from Trent which told Orlov all he needed to know. Ignoring Trent's further shouts he moved closer and slowly ran the point of his blade along my jaw line as he spoke softly, intimately, to me.

"So, you are Trent's woman. Now that is very...appealing."

I glared back at him silently. My arm stung. Blood soaked through my shirt, my jacket. I could see the dark stain spreading and willed it to stop.

Gloating now, Orlov spoke to Trent. "Fiery, isn't she? I can see it in her eyes, her desire to kill me."

"Emma, do nothing to antagonise him," Trent ordered harshly, and I could tell from his voice he was on the move. I remembered Orlov had told them where we were, and was surprised. Why would Orlov want to draw them to him? Surely it'd be easier for them to escape in a vehicle if there were as few people here as possible? It didn't make sense.

"Emma," Orlov repeated softly, managing to make it sound threatening. His face was too close to mine, and as I fought my nausea and fear he continued, this time all business. "It sounds as if you're on your way here, Trent. Put Cavendish on."

Cavendish did not wait to hear what Orlov wanted, but told him firmly, "I want to make an exchange, Orlov. Me in place of my family. I'm on my way to the Manor now."

"We will agree to that," Orlov replied. He swopped knowing looks with Ugly, and my heart sank. It was clear there would be no exchange. They wanted to kidnap the full set.

Grace saw the exchange too, and she yelled, "It's a trap, Henry, they will never let..." She was brutally silenced by the butt of Ugly's gun. The speed and violence of the blow was startling and she dropped to the floor, unconscious. The children screamed as they saw their mother fall and moved closer to me, clutching at my clothes, seeking reassurance. I tried to hold myself together from the shock of the violent attack on Grace and comforted them. As I did I felt Sophia's cold little hand prise my fingers open and push a hard object into my palm.

Orlov did not react to Ugly's attack on Grace. Without responding to the shouts coming from Cavendish, he ended the call and slipped my phone into his pocket. Then he made another call, using his own phone. I knelt, trying to see if Grace was okay, but with my hands tied behind my back there was little I could do other than reassure the children and look for any signs that she was waking up. Blood trickled from her temple, staining her hair, and I hoped she was merely unconscious.

Orlov and Ugly were becoming more animated now in their conversation. They checked their watches and appeared to be getting ready to leave.

Looking up from where I knelt on the ground, I interrupted their mutterings. "They'll be here any minute, and you'll never get away. Any vehicle you take will be stopped and you are outnumbered."

Orlov smiled the confident smile of one who knows something you don't, and sounded almost dismissive as he spoke. "We will be gone before they even get back."

It was then that I heard it, coming from above: a droning engine. A plane? Surely not. There wasn't the space for one to land here. A helicopter then? My stomach plummeted. This was actually happening; we really were going to be taken, and no one was going to be able to do anything about it. The children looked over at me, and I tried to reassure them that it would be all right as the droning grew louder and louder, and within moments passed directly overhead, sounding closer and closer like it was coming lower, like it was coming in to land.

Orlov and Ugly moved quickly. Ugly picked up Grace's body and almost effortlessly flung her over his shoulder. Her head lolled down his back, her arms swinging awkwardly because of being tied. He jerked his gun to tell the children to stand and come close to him. Then they all moved towards the front door.

Orlov took up his position behind me, holding me unpleasantly close, his arm around my waist this time as he pressed himself against me. My hands were tied and positioned at a place where I could have caused him maximum pain, but with the others at risk I couldn't take the chance. I'd seen he carried a gun: it was tucked in the back of his trousers, but he seemed to prefer the knife. I felt its sharp edge against the skin of my neck. My phone rang and he took the knife away as he reached to answer it, his other arm tightening on my waist as if warning me not to take advantage of the situation. He must have put the knife away somewhere to answer – I thought perhaps now was the moment, but I'd seen how quick he was with it.

112

My arm throbbed as a reminder, and even if I did manage to overcome him, a big if, there was also Ugly to deal with, and the fact that my hands were still tied.

With Orlov's head so close to mine as he answered the call I could hear Trent's voice anyway, but Orlov obligingly flicked it on to loudspeaker so I got the full benefit of Trent's threats as to what he would do to him if he hurt me.

"I have no intention of hurting her, Trent. I'm very much looking forward to making her mine. Among other things, Trent, we share the same taste in women. I can feel her body against mine, firm as I like it, but soft in all the right places." My flesh crawled with fear. "Of course, I can't be held responsible for what will happen when I have had enough of her and give her to my boys."

I knew he was smiling as he taunted Trent and I didn't want to think about what my future might hold.

"I'm coming to get you, Emma." Trent's words were fiercely spoken, though futile, knowing what I knew and he didn't. Then his tone turned deadly. "And you, Orlov." The phone went dead.

Orlov chuckled behind me. "Ah, Emma, life with me won't be so very different, you know. Trent and I, we are like the same."

"He is nothing like you, he would never behave like you do," I spat.

His voice came back roughly. "Oh, don't kid yourself, Emma, he is just like me, and he behaves just like me. You are a fool if you don't believe that."

As we caught up with the others, the chest was pushed to the side and the door opened as Orlov looked to check all was clear. I tried to pull my head back to give someone the chance to blow his off, but no one did. I couldn't believe they were going to be able to walk out of here, though I guessed it was hardly likely anyone would take a chance on shooting with us being used as shields.

We stepped out into the wall of sound that came from the aircraft, although we couldn't see it yet, and started towards the way out of the courtyard. Dawn was coming; it was still a long way off, but the depth of colour in the sky had lightened. I could hear the whip of the blades turning, the sound increasing as we passed through the entrance, and I gasped as I took my first look at the strangest aircraft I'd ever seen. Its grey body was shaped like that of a large helicopter, but it had plane-like wings attached in one long spread across the top of the fuselage. On the end of each wing was mounted a large vertical distorted ovoid like a misshapen pod with a set of shortened helicopter blades fixed to the top. I'd never seen such a thing before.

I watched as Ugly, carrying Grace, herded the children along in front of us. Panic rose in me as I tried to resist, my heels digging in, scuffing up gravel and dirt as I scrabbled for purchase. Orlov, feeling my resistance, increased the hold he had on me. My hands, balled into fists, were uncomfortably trapped between our bodies, the cable tie biting into my skin, my shoulders strained from having my hands tied behind me. He forced me towards the plane, lifting my feet from the ground as he half-carried me, still struggling, cursing as he growled in my ear, "Be still."

As we approached the side steps, the back of the plane started opening, gaping as if it yawned. I tried to watch what was happening, but Orlov kept my head tipped to one side with the knife at my throat. I could only see from the corner of my eye, but it was enough, and I saw a body as it tumbled out of the gap and fell heavily on to the grass. There was no further movement. A sob caught in my throat in horror as Orlov continued, against my renewed struggles, in his battle to get me on the plane.

And then I saw him. Trent. I saw him as he leapt out of the pickup even before it came to a halt inside the treeline.

A silhouette against the headlights that I would recognise anywhere, closely followed by others who dashed to catch him when he didn't stop. They grabbed his arms as he lunged towards me, and held him back under the protection of the trees. Even from this distance I could feel his fury. My own anger rose up in reaction to Orlov's chuckle, his hot breath against my neck. I willed Trent to stay put, to stay safe.

We'd reached the steps. Ugly had already taken Grace and the children through the doorway and I continued to make life difficult for Orlov by bracing my feet against the steps. Orlov had had enough. I felt the sting of his blade slicing through the skin of my neck, the sharp pain bringing tears to my eyes as I cried out. My legs weakened and Orlov seized the opportunity to force me through the door and into the bare shell of a plane. Grey and utilitarian, it was fitted with a row of basic bench-type seating down each side. Ugly had taken Grace and the children to the furthest bench, and Grace had been laid out along the seating, a lap belt round her waist to keep her in place. I saw him roughly push each of the children on to the bench next to her, and they sat, pale and frightened.

Orlov ordered me to sit on the bench opposite and I did so. There was little point in resisting now. My arm was throbbing and my neck stung where he'd cut me, but I was pleased to see by his laboured breathing that he'd had to exert himself manhandling me on to the plane. I knew there was still a glimmer of hope for us because he had my phone in his pocket and we could be tracked from that. But as if he'd read my thoughts, he pulled the phone out of his pocket, and threw it out of the door before slamming it closed. He hadn't taken his eyes off me throughout, and now smiled at the disappointment I couldn't hide.

That was that then. The fight went out of me and my head dropped in despair. He crouched on his haunches in front of me, his knees each side of mine as he lifted my chin. I tried not to flinch away from him as he murmured, "Never mind, Emma, you can forget Trent. Now you are mine, and I know how to look after you." He reached out to me. I did flinch this time, but he merely picked up the two halves of my lap belt and clicked them closed across my lap. Then he stood up and crossed to the small door at the front. Glancing back, his eyes met mine briefly, then defeated I looked away, dropping my gaze before he disappeared into the cockpit, satisfied, knowing I was beaten.

But it would be a long time before I was that.

# Chapter 9

The light was dim in the enclosed space, the air damp and cold. I looked over at the children, trying to give them a comforting smile. "It's all right," I lied, "your Dad and Trent and all the others are going to come and find us. We'll be fine." I hoped I sounded more convincing than I felt. They didn't respond. I told them how to do up their lap belts, which gave them something to do for a few moments, but they were soon still again and there was nothing more I could think of.

Ugly was staying with us, which was a shame. He'd taken up a standing position by the cockpit door as soon as Orlov had passed through it, and almost immediately I heard the engine noise increase, and as we started to lift from the ground I slumped back on the bench. Struggling with Orlov had caused me to break out in a sweat again, but already I was cooling, the chill of the air stripping the heat from my body. The cable tie had bitten into the skin of my wrists as I'd fought against Orlov, and I could feel my skin chafed and stinging as sweat mingled with blood. I unclamped my fingers from around the object Sophia had forced into my hand, having to clench and unclench the fingers of alternate hands to force movement back into them. By the feel of it, I recognised the object as one of the multitools I had given to the children for Christmas. Sophia was looking at me, and checking Ugly wasn't watching I mouthed at her, "Well done!" I was pleased to see the glimmer of a smile touch her lips.

In the handle of the multitool was a blade, and I tried to ease it out of its casing. My fingers were slippery, though I wasn't sure what with, hoping for sweat rather than blood.

Trying to stay still and appear as if I was behaving myself for Ugly's sake, my fingers worked as quickly as they could. I got the blade out, then turned the tool in my hand until I was sure I had the blade up against the cable tie. Though it was at an awkward angle, I started moving my hand up and down, concentrating on the task of cutting through. I had to rest every couple of minutes because my hand kept cramping. I had to stretch it out, wiggle my fingers, and then find the place where I'd started to make a notch and start again, unable to put as much force against the cable as I wanted to because of the angle I had to hold it. After what felt like an excruciatingly long time I suddenly felt the tie loosen. I managed to catch and hold it in my fingers so it didn't drop through the gap in the seat to the floor and give me away. I sat for a moment before folding the blade away, and tucked the tool and the cable tie into the top of my jodhpurs. Now I needed to bide my time. I surreptitiously looked around to see what I had at my disposal. It wasn't a lot. Unsurprisingly everything was bolted down, and there wasn't a handy supply of obvious weapons available. I would have to be creative.

I kept my arms behind me, flexing my wrists and hands while I watched Ugly. The engine noise in our section was a loud continual droning. I could feel the reverberations of the engines coming through the floor, and although it had always been cold in here, it was now getting colder. The aircraft looked like it was used for troop transportation and there didn't appear to be much by way of insulation or any other comforts. I wondered how long we would be flying for. I wondered who else would be in the cockpit beside Orlov. I thought there would probably only be one. Three of them in all. My timing would have to be good.

I'd kept a close eye on Grace and saw the first signs of her coming round. Her eyelids flickered, then opened quickly and widened in alarm as she tried to make sense of where she was. The children realised she was awake,

Sophia crying as she tried to hug her. Grace took in the noise, the vibration, the cold. She groaned as she tried to sit up too quickly, struggling in her attempts to do so with her hands tied. I mouthed the words "Are you all right?" She nodded vacantly, still pretty much out of it. She looked around, saw Ugly, her eyes flicking away from him, and automatically comforted the children who cuddled up close. I closed my eyes, feeling a sudden pang of loss and of being alone.

We'd been flying for perhaps half an hour when Ugly suddenly turned and pulled open the cockpit door. It appeared he'd been summoned, though how he could have heard anyone calling over the level of noise in this small space was beyond me. The door blocked me from his sight as he leaned into the cockpit, and I took my chance. I leapt up, my legs unsteady as I grabbed the small fire extinguisher, ripping it out of the strapping that held it beside the door, and moved towards Ugly, standing behind him so as to be ready. With all we'd already been through, I felt weak and concerned I wouldn't have enough strength. There would be no second chances – he would be on me in a shot, and that thought alone was enough to make me feel like jelly. My reactions were slow, and so deep was I in my thoughts I almost missed the moment. Whatever exchange he'd been having with the pilots had ended. He'd withdrawn his head from the doorway and was closing the door. I waited until it clicked shut, then brought the fire extinguisher smashing down on the back of his head. Nothing happened. He just froze. Oh God, I hadn't hit him hard enough! Then, almost in slow motion, his knees collapsed and he fell like a tree in a forest, out cold.

I worked quickly, taking his gun away, then checking through his pockets. I found a bundle of cable ties, and it was satisfying to bind his wrists and ankles, drag him across the floor and use more ties to attach him to the struts under the bench seats opposite Grace and the children.

I went over to the others. Grace was looking a little brighter, and I hugged Sophia and Reuben who were more responsive now, though they looked tearstained and exhausted. I cut the cable tie binding Grace's hands, and after rubbing her wrists and moving her shoulders to ease the stiffness, she used one hand to steady herself. The other she brought to her head, which must have been pounding, and carefully felt her wound, the blood encrusted in her hair. I told them all to try and keep warm, then filled them in on my plan. Grace hugged the children closer to her, and I gave them the job of keeping an eye on Ugly.

I had no idea how the next part of my plan would work out, but I couldn't think of any other option, so I picked up the fire extinguisher again and stood ready behind the cockpit door, hoping that someone would eventually come through it.

I waited, and waited, becoming more and more impatient, knowing that with every moment that passed that we were travelling further and further from home. I wondered what would happen if I forced the situation and went into the cockpit. Could I deal with both men before one of them disabled me? I didn't think it was a feasible solution, but the thoughts and plans kept going round and round in my head.

Shouts came from the other side of the door. Startled, I realised that in my exhaustion I'd nearly fallen asleep on my feet and missed the moment I'd been waiting for: the moment where Ugly would be wanted, and when he didn't come, someone would come looking for him. It was simple. The best plans always were. What could possibly go wrong? I asked myself.

More shouts, and I stood ready, thinking of the timing, the door opening, hoping whoever came through it wouldn't turn as they closed the door and see me. I braced myself as I saw the handle move. The door flew open. Whoever was coming through it was not happy. He stopped abruptly, slamming the door shut, seeing Grace and the children who sat up straight, alarmed at his entrance. Before he had a chance to see Ugly, I hit him, with the same result. He toppled and fell at the feet of Grace and the children.

It wasn't Orlov, which was a pity. I didn't really want to have to confront him, and that was the next part of the plan, but putting that out of my mind for the moment I bound my second victim of the night and relieved him of his gun.

I had a couple of weapons to choose from now, but had no idea which would be the best to use, or even if either of them had any bullets in them. Having nothing else to go on I went with eeny meeny miny mo before picking the bigger and heavier one, hoping I wouldn't have to fire it.

The children gave me thumbs up signs, and I was spurred on. Grace asked if she could do anything to help, and while I admired and was encouraged by her determination, she was in no condition for action so I shook my head. Turning to face the door, I took a deep breath and grabbed the handle. I opened it as sharply as the last man had, stepped inside and closed it firmly behind me. Ignoring everything else, I focused on Orlov, who barked out something which sounded like a curse, but he didn't bother to turn round, so confident was he that we had all been neutralised. I stood still, holding the gun like I'd seen tough people do in films, two-handed and straight-armed, hoping I looked more confident than I felt and that my rigid stance would stop my knees shaking. My hands were clammy on the gun.

Obviously wondering why his co-pilot hadn't taken his seat, Orlov glanced back. His eyes widened as he saw me, then, quickly regaining his composure, he said calmly, "It seems I underestimated you, Emma."

"Yes...and now you are mine." I hoped my voice didn't come out as weak and feeble as I was feeling. It sounded okay.

"What are you expecting of me?"

"I'm expecting you to turn this plane around and return to Melton."

"I can't do that."

"I can make you do that." I waved the gun slightly as if maybe he hadn't noticed I was holding it.

"You think so? I don't, Emma. I don't think you would fire that in here. That would be dangerous for all of you."

I thought about it. I'd heard of people being sucked out of planes when windows were broken. Was that true, or merely a myth? I didn't know, and didn't want to find out. I tried one last time.

"Turn the plane around."

"No." He hesitated, as if coming to a decision before continuing, and he sounded resigned. "Emma, you don't know the people I work for. I can't return without the hostages. If I turned round now that would be seen as a failure and certain death for me. So, I either continue on our fixed course or...if you force the situation I take this plane down, and at least my death will be at my own hand."

Shock was not the word for what I felt then. I hadn't anticipated the fact that Grace, the children and I were trapped in a plane with a suicidal madman. As my great plan splintered around me, I saw his hand move, reaching for something. A weapon? I lunged at him, yelling "Neither scenario works for me," and whacked him on the side of the head. It wasn't like taking out the others with the extinguisher – that had seemed at a distance, somehow. Now up close I could feel the heat of his body, his hair on

122

my fingers as the gun made contact once, twice...and he was still.

Shaking, I collapsed to my knees, nausea rising as I retched, my poor empty stomach unable to provide anything to throw up.

What the hell was I going to do now? I hadn't imagined this ending at all. In my happy-ever-after, Orlov was going to fly us all back home safely and then be locked away forever.

No time to dwell on that now. I needed to get a grip, and I struggled back to my exhausted feet. Quick assessment: unconscious man in cockpit but plane still flying as if nothing had happened, so I reasoned it must be on autopilot. We were therefore okay for the time being. Second quick assessment: Grace, though willing, was not yet with it; quite understandable, but not particularly helpful in the current situation. The children were, of course, children, and therefore not of much help with what was needed. So that left me to sort this out. The responsibility I'd felt all night continued to weigh heavy.

First things first: get Orlov out of the cockpit. It would be tough, but I didn't want him in there. Even if I tied him up, it would be distracting if he regained consciousness. I removed the headset he was wearing and put it down on his far side. Reaching across him I released his harness and pulled it down over his arms. Standing behind his seat, I put my hands under his armpits, and then shoved my arms under before wrapping them across his chest as I locked my hands together, his head lolling against mine. I braced myself, then hauled with all my might, feeling his body lift, getting it on to the armrest. I suddenly felt resistance and stopped to regain my breath. Taking the weight of his upper body across my chest I reached under him, feeling along the armrest. His pocket had snared on the end. I released it, then stood back up and took the strain again. His body came towards me in a rush now he was over the

123

pivotal point, his backside crashing to the floor, his legs following, floppy and long. If this treatment didn't wake him up, I didn't know what would. I had to tie him up as quickly as possible. I dragged him to the door, kicking it wide as I pulled him through before depositing him on the floor. Collapsing to my knees beside him, I gasped for breath as my chest heaved with the effort.

Looking up I caught three startled faces staring at me. This was not the plan, they knew that. I tried to explain and reassure them that everything would be fine. I tried not to meet their eyes. I used extra ties on Orlov to make sure he was going nowhere, and remembered to separate him from his knife. At last I was done and went over to Grace. She tried to stand but I stopped her, bending to her level and hugging her tightly for a moment, tears coming to my eyes which I tried to blink away.

I whispered in her ear, "I don't suppose there's any chance you know how to..." and I couldn't bring myself to finish the sentence. I felt her shake her head against my shoulder. It had always been unlikely, but I had to ask. Then I released her and hugged each of the children before encouraging them to sit back down and strap themselves in tightly with their lap-straps.

Sophia, dirty and exhausted, her voice tight with emotion, asked, "Do you know what you're doing? Do you know how to fly?"

"Absolutely," I reassured her, not trusting my voice to stay firm enough to say anything further as I smiled at them all before turning and heading back to the yawning door that led to the cockpit, closing it firmly behind me.

# Chapter 10

I climbed into the seat recently vacated by Orlov and fastened the four-point safety harness around me, trying to put off the moment when I would have to think about the huge mess I was in. When I was fully secure I looked out of the cockpit window and took in the view of the beautiful dawn sky as soft pinks merged with deeper purples. The early morning sun was making its first appearance, shyly casting warm golden fingers over a waking earth. The sky was lightening and in time looked likely to become a solid blue, the few puffs of cloud present unlikely to survive the heat the sun was promising. Well, I thought, feeling a little light-headed, it's a lovely day for it. I couldn't face what the "it" might be, and I didn't look down.

I picked up the headset and pulled it on until it settled comfortably over my ears. Not knowing what to do, I rather hesitantly called "Mayday, Mayday, Mayday" into the mouthpiece. I jumped as I heard a woman's voice.

"This is Area Radar, we are receiving you loud and clear. Confirm squawk identity. Over."

"I don't know what that is. My name is Emma Grayson, and I'm in a plane. I don't know what sort it is or where I am, but we've been taken hostage. By 'we' I mean me and Grace...sorry Lady Cavendish and her children, and now I've taken over the plane but I'm not a pilot...Over?" I made it sound like a question as I wasn't sure if I was meant to end with that or not, but thought I'd follow her lead. I also realised I was gabbling and wondered what my mystery voice would make of it.

"State location of pilot. Over."

"He's tied up in the back. I knocked him out and now I need help. Over." I was getting the hang of it.

"Why did you knock him out? Over."

"He was threatening to crash the plane because he wouldn't take us where we wanted to go. Over."

Silence filled the airwaves as I waited, feeling better for having made some contact with the outside world.

"Grayson, you are flying a Victor Two Two Osprey aircraft. We are tracking you on radar. Over."

Relief flowed through me that at least they knew where we were. "You should know I'm not flying this plane. It's on autopilot and I'm sitting in it. There is no pilot on board who is conscious and I need help. Over."

"Grayson, stand by. I will come back to you."

At least there wasn't any music to listen to. The silence was total and stretched out interminably, though in reality she was probably back within thirty seconds.

"Grayson, jets are scrambled to intercept and will be with you shortly. I say again, help is on its way. Over."

"Thank you!"

Hugely relieved at the thought that help was on the way, I thought I'd better familiarise myself with the controls. I had to face the fact that I was going to have to fly the plane. My stomach lurched at the prospect.

"Grayson?" Her tone softer now.

"Yes," I muttered, stomach lurching as I tried to concentrate on the dials in front of me.

"Would you like to talk to me until help arrives?"

"Thanks, but I'm going to use the time to find my way round the controls. Don't go far though, will you?"

"I'll be right here."

Time to get to work. I stared at the dials in front of me. I needed to give myself something to do. The harness restrained my body as I rocked against it, back and forth, back and forth. I didn't want to think about how high up we were. I'd never had a particular problem with heights, but there are heights and then there are *heights*, and this situation involved the latter.

I tried to concentrate on the task in hand. Looking out of the cockpit, I noticed that the misshapen pods on the end of the wings had turned through ninety degrees, so that what had previously looked like helicopter blades were now like the propeller blades on a plane.

I brought my attention back to the cockpit. Focusing on the controls around me, I tried to think practically. I could drive, so how much harder could this be? There was a big open sky – and all I had to worry about was not hitting the ground. I peered at the dials in front of me, skittering from one to another. Most of the dials made no sense to me, though several of them had labels under them which were useful. The labels were strips of red plastic with the letters punched into them, and I recalled one of my foster-fathers, an engineer of some sort, having a machine that made these, and I remembered getting into a lot of trouble one day when I'd used it to punch out all the rude words I knew.

I leant forward and peered at these labels. I found the fuel gauge and was reassured to see it registered at over three quarters full. The autopilot button was similarly marked. I'd seen enough films to know the main controlling thing was the joystick bit immediately in front of me and between my legs, but, as I looked at the other dials, labelled or otherwise, I didn't think they were going to be of any help at all.

"Hello, Em." Trent's voice, deep in my ears, was like silk flowing over my shattered nerves, soothing and comforting. My eyes closed and I exhaled, letting my head drop back against the headrest.

"Hello," I mumbled, feeling overcome and close to tears.

"I bet your heart is beating that little bit faster now, isn't it?"

I couldn't help but smile as I was reminded of a conversation we'd had the previous year when he'd caught me galloping on the stubble.

"I prefer my own controllable thrills," I said.

"Open your eyes, Em...look at me."

*Look at me?* My eyes jolted open. I looked around. There he was, out of my side window, a little lower than me in the rear seat of a jet. I narrowed my eyes, trying to see if it really was him. He pushed up his blacked-out visor and grinned at me. I sat staring, open-mouthed. Well, of course he would be able to fly, wouldn't he, though the thought had never crossed my mind before. I heard myself say feebly, and somewhat unnecessarily, "You can fly?" I'd always assumed it was Cavendish that flew the Apache. I'd never thought further than that.

"Yes, Em, though technically I'm not actually flying. That's being done by my RAF friend in front. Sadly my days of flying planes like these are over."

"Is it just you?"

"Why...am I suddenly not enough for you?" he teased lightly. "Sorry, probably not the right time for levity. No, Cavendish is on the way. I left him with the paperwork, plus he's always been a bit slow off the mark."

The banter felt good, as if I wasn't in a precarious situation at all. His voice softened as he asked, "How badly are you hurt, Em?"

I brushed it off. "I'm fine. A little battered and bruised, but nothing serious. And you?...What happened?"

"I'm fine...I'll fill you in when we've more time."

Seconds later I heard, "Morning, Tiger." I looked over to see Cavendish on my other side, and put my hand up to wave. "How's the family?"

"They're fine. Grace is conscious again, but still a little weak. The children are obviously scared, but they're okay." This brought my situation home to me. I swallowed with some difficulty and asked, "Can you get us down from here?" I sounded pathetic.

"Of course we can. There's no problem with that, Em." And Trent was so positive it lifted my spirits immediately, though I still wasn't sure how it was going to be possible.

"But...how? I don't know how to fly this thing."

"Flying is quite straightforward, Em. We'll keep it basic, I'll talk you through it."

Straightforward? That seemed unlikely, but I let out a deep breath. "Okay...let's get on with it then."

"That's my girl."

Trent chuckled as Cavendish said, "Grayson, I'm going to leave Trent to guide you so as not to confuse you, but I'm here if you need me."

"Thanks, Cavendish."

"Okay, Grayson," Trent began, "let's get you home. I'm going to give you a guided tour of the basics. The joystick in front of you does all the steering of the plane. Left and right are obvious, push it forward for down and pull it back towards you for up. So we're going to have a practice by turning this aircraft around."

"That's all you're going to tell me?"

"That's all you need to know for now – I told you it was simple. Can you see the switch in front of you marked 'autopilot'?"

"Yes."

"Flick it off, and you'll feel a change through the joystick as soon as you take control."

I leant across and gingerly flicked the switch. The plane dipped suddenly. My stomach followed suit.

"Very gently, Grayson, pull the joystick a little towards you and lift her up."

I followed his instructions, surprised at how responsive the controls were. I felt better once we were back on what felt like an even keel again.

"That's great. Okay, time to turn around, Grayson."

129

"What about you? I don't want to hit either of you."

"Don't worry about us, we'll keep out of your way."

Okay then, I thought, time to make my first manoeuvre. I swung the joystick to the left. The plane reacted far quicker than I thought it would, banking round at a steep angle. Out of my window I saw the jet swoop out of the way as we went into a nosedive.

Trent spoke quickly. "Steady there, Grayson, a little lighter on the controls. Ease back on the joystick to bring the nose back up."

"Okay," I said shakily. I did as he said, the plane levelling out as we turned in a wider circle. I took a deep breath, found the sun behind us, and levelled off again when told to do so. I felt considerably better once I was pointing in the direction of home, and pleased to see Trent and Cavendish back in position on either side of me. They might not have been able to help physically, but I felt safer having them there as my escorts.

"Well done, Emma" came the warm voice again. I risked a quick look over at him and he gave me a thumbs-up. I smiled to myself. I can do this, I thought, though that was tempered with another that lurked in the back of my mind. Don't think about what's to come.

I needed to relax, but couldn't. Though I was exhausted with exertion and lack of sleep, my body was as taut as a piano wire. I could feel the stiffness and tension through my arms, shoulders and back. My head pounded from dehydration, lack of sleep and the knocks it had received. The skin around one eye was tight and swollen. I could feel blood encrusted along my eyebrow, and on my skin where it had run down my face. The arm of my jacket was soaked through with blood, though I no longer appeared to be bleeding, and I could feel my clothes sticking to the knife-wound as the blood dried in the chill of the cockpit. My flesh was bruised black and purple around the wound in my leg. I was filthy, stinking and tired beyond belief.

"You okay, Emma? You've gone quiet on me." Trent's anxious voice woke me from my dazed state.

I was afraid of asking the question, but I had to know. "How is everyone?" I faltered.

"Everyone's fine, Em,"

Really? Could that honestly be true?

"Carlton?" I'd left him behind, a decision he hadn't even questioned.

"He's fine. He's waiting for us back at Loreley."

"Back at where?" I frowned.

"RAF Loreley, it's the closest station to Melton. It's where we flew out of. Do you remember, Em? Do you remember me telling you we had a small transport aircraft?"

I did. "This is it? Your aircraft?"

"Yes. We have a hanger on the station."

"Then where's Turner? You said Turner flew this plane."

"Yes. They targeted Turner, Em. They used him to get them on to the estate, then we believe they took him off to arrange access to RAF Loreley. He must have filed a flight plan, made it all legitimate, otherwise an aircraft being taken would be shot down immediately. Ideally they needed him, though any one of us pilots would have sufficed."

A flash of an image came to me, seen from the corner of my eye. The back of the aircraft opening, a body rolled up and out of the gap, hitting the ground heavily and not moving. "Oh my God," I gasped, "oh my God, Trent – Turner?"

"Yes, they dropped him when they'd finished with him..."

Not giving him time to explain, I butted in. "And is he...is he...?" I couldn't bring myself to finish the question.

"He's alive, Em, but in bad shape. In time he'll be fine."

131

"And Porter?" My voice was barely more than a whisper as I remembered his falling body.

"Also fine," Trent reassured me. "There are a few injuries, Em, I won't lie, but that's all, and none of them life-threatening. We'll have a full debrief when we get you home."

I was surprised the estate could have held out against such an attack without losing anyone, and I hoped he wasn't just telling me what I wanted to hear, but I was going to have to deal with that later. We were on a steady course now and I needed to know what was coming up.

He interrupted my thoughts again. "Em, you okay? Shall we talk about something else?"

"I'm fine, I need to keep focused, that's all. How much longer is it before we're back?"

"Another half an hour or so."

"Okay...Start telling me how to land this thing."

"We could leave it a while yet."

"No, tell me now so I can think it through." I heard his resigned sigh, but knew he wouldn't refuse.

He told me how I would have to raise the turbo-prop engines to helicopter mode, by using the lever to my left, explaining how this would allow the plane's avionics to keep it steady as we descended slowly. Then he instructed me on reducing the engine power and how to approach a vertical landing. He talked me through it all once: what I'd see ahead of me on the runway, what to aim for, how to lower the undercarriage, how to bring the plane down while keeping its nose up, how to reduce speed while still flying and what to do once on the ground.

I couldn't wait to get there, impatient to feel this beast come to a stop beneath me. Trent came to the end of his explanation and I made him repeat it, running through it again, and again. I'd felt the weight of the plane now in my hands, I knew how it felt to control it. As Trent ran through the instructions again I closed my eyes, imagining the landing, how it would feel as we touched down. I ran through each instruction in my mind, my fuzzy brain almost hallucinating, the images, the feelings so vividly real that, as I opened my eyes, disappointment washed over me because we weren't already on the tarmac. The instructions ran as if on a loop, over and over in my mind, overlapping with Trent's words. Then in the distance I realised I could see the runway.

I had to do this one thing, this one last thing, and it would all be over and I could sleep forever, I thought. My exhausted mind started to wander, bringing thoughts of my angel. I imagined her with me, sitting with me. I could picture her as clearly as if she'd never left me, smiling and warm and waiting for me. Home already, I thought, smiling at Eva. Flashing blue lights highlighted the runway. They looked like fairy lights in the hazy dawn air, but I realised they were the lights of the fire engines, the police cars and ambulances lined up in readiness for a catastrophe.

Eva disappeared as it suddenly hit me that this was not a game or some form of make believe. I really was going to have to do this. And I couldn't. My hands and fingers gripped the control stick with all their might, my arms rigid as the words ran through my mind. I can't do this, I can't do this, I can't do this. I began gasping as panic seized me. Tears wet my face and I clamped one hand to my mouth, trying to stifle the sound...I can't do this, I can't do this, I can't do this...not realising I was saying it out loud.

My panic was broken by Trent barking, "Grayson! Snap out of it, do you hear me? Come back to me. Grayson! Answer me!" His demands were loud and clear as I gasped, my head spinning as I tried to focus on his words.

"Grayson, control your breathing and you will control your fear, I promise you. Do as I say, now. Take a deep breath..." I inhaled as deeply as I could "...and let it out slowly." I let it out, my chest shuddering, then I took in another breath and exhaled it again, trying to steady myself. The runway loomed ahead.

"Thank God, Emma...that's better, calmer." I could hear his sigh of relief through the headset. His voice was steady again. "Okay. We're going to do a circle round before attempting the landing."

I wiped my eyes and wet cheeks with the heel of my hand. All I wanted to do was land and get this over with, but I croaked a feeble "Okay" into the mouthpiece. Flying onwards, Trent led me round in a large circle. He used the time to soothe me, to get my mindset as close to being in the right place as it was possible to be before lining me up again on the approach. I tried to gather my thoughts again, but I was beyond being capable of that. I glanced anxiously across at Cavendish and Trent, acknowledging the thumbs ups they gave me. Then I looked forward and took a deep breath.

The jets disappeared from my side. Trent had explained they would have to leave me to make sure I didn't get caught in their jet-stream, but he didn't stop talking to me, guiding me in, repeating his earlier instructions, calmly correcting my approach as I ignored the flashing lights, the onlookers, the audience. I said a silent prayer to a God I no longer believed in as I followed every direction. I thought of the precious cargo I was carrying and the man waiting for me.

The plane shuddered as I brought it in. It lurched as I tried to correct the descent, tried to keep it even, overcorrecting one way, then the other, my mouth dry. There was a jolt as the wheels hit the tarmac too hard, bouncing back off and coming down again more gently until finally, finally, finally we stopped, and it was over.

"Don't move, Emma, I'm coming to get you."

I couldn't have moved if I'd tried. Frozen in place with fear, even the relief at finally coming to a standstill was not enough to thaw me. Vehicles started to surround us, blue lights flashing as they came into view, people spilling out on to the tarmac. I watched the jets touch down further up the runway then turn and taxi back, stopping so I could see the passengers leap out and run.

I'd already heard a commotion coming from the back, the door being pulled open, people clattering up the steps, but I didn't look back.

Trent appeared at my shoulder with soft words to warm me as he prised my hands from the control stick. He removed the headset and undid my harness before lifting me from my seat as if I weighed nothing. People were filling the rear section. I saw Cavendish hugging his family and others hunched over the prisoners as Trent carried me through the cabin and out of the door, chilly early morning air hitting my face.

Coming down the steps I was vaguely aware of people, vehicles, flashing lights around us. People with questions pushed forward as I buried myself in Trent's chest, and he ignored it all, intent only on reaching his truck. Then he kissed my cheek, murmuring that he'd be back shortly. I was shocked that he was leaving me. I desperately felt the need to cling to him and not let him go, but he lowered me to the ground and I stood on shaking legs.

"Keep her warm, make her drink and don't leave her," he commanded, then turned and walked off.

Someone wrapped a blanket round my shoulders. I looked up to see Carlton, remembering Trent had said he'd be waiting. He opened the rear door of the truck, helping me up and on to the seat before handing me a bottle of water. Then he climbed up beside me, wrapping me in his arms as he held me close.

I'd not taken my eyes off Trent's passage back through the gathered throng, and I watched him now as he talked animatedly with the police, hands firmly planted on his hips when he wasn't gesticulating. He was not looking happy at all. I sipped at the water. I was so thirsty I wanted to gulp it down, but didn't trust my stomach to hold on to it for long if I did.

"The horses are all okay, Em. They're back in the stables. Greene, Burton and Young went to get them earlier." He told me what he knew I wanted to know, but I couldn't reply. I resorted instead to freeing my hand from the folds of blanket and taking his in mine as I held him tightly. Satisfied with this we sat, my head in the hollow of his shoulder as he rested his cheek against my hair, not seeming to care how filthy it was.

Trent was back within minutes, and after asking Carlton to drive he came and held me. I curled into his chest, only waking as we drove into the yard. Four heads over the stable doors were all I needed to see as Trent helped me out. As I walked unsteadily towards the cottage Susie threw herself at me, and I collapsed to my knees as I took her in my arms and held her close, my face buried in her coat.

Stanton and Bray were waiting in the kitchen for me. They told me I might feel some discomfort as they dealt with my wounds. I felt nothing. My split eyebrow was cleaned, the edges held together with butterfly stitches, my neck wound similarly treated. My jacket and shirt were cut from me, the cloth soaked and eased gently away from the laceration on my arm which stung and continued to ooze blood until it was anaesthetised and stitched. Bray checked the rest of me, cutting away my jodphurs as she cleaned the flesh wound. While they worked they chatted, trying to put me at ease, but I wasn't able to respond. I was as though an invisible wall was shutting me off from what was going on around me. When both were satisfied nothing further needed attending to, they left us with dressings for the wounds to be put on once I'd been in the bath that had been run by Trent.

I ate the toast put in front of me and drank disgustingly sweet tea, which I'd thought was an old wives' tale, and heard promises made of more to eat later when I'd feel more like it. Just as well – it was all I could do to keep the toast down.

Soon Trent and I were on our own, and I went through to the sitting room to see the damage. Most of the panes in the window had been broken. The office was the same. The walls were pockmarked by bullets, and I wondered how Carlton had survived.

Then Trent took me upstairs, helping me to undress before I stepped into the deep, warm bath. He washed me as if I were a child, shampooing my hair, his fingers gently massaging my scalp, then rinsing the dirt and soap away. Then he soaped the rest of me, soothingly caressing my skin before he joined me in the bath. Getting out, we wrapped ourselves in big, fluffy towels, and I put a hand on his shoulder, my fingers touching the skin already darkened to purple-black, matching the bruises on his ribs. I checked over his beautiful body, taking in a wound on his leg, another on his arm. He stopped my hand, covering it with his as I looked at him, and he murmured, "It's okay...I'm okay," then, kissing me softly, he led me to the bedroom, drying my hair before putting me to bed. I lay shivering, despite the heat of the day, and unable to close my eyes until he'd crawled in behind me, curling his warm body around mine. I fell asleep feeling his protection surround me.

We woke as the sun was going down; long fingers of pink streaked the sky as night closed in on the day we'd missed. Sleepy and tousle-haired, we ate tomato and basil soup that had been left for us, together with thick doorsteps of fresh white thickly buttered bread which melted deliciously into the soup when dunked, adding to the creamy richness. This was followed by a pasta dish that I picked at while Trent ate ravenously, both of us feeling better as we replenished our bodies with goodness and energy. We ate in silence, neither needing to talk. I couldn't. I hadn't spoken since landing. Trent accepted this, not asking anything as he took me back to bed and we crashed out again.

I woke in the night, gasping as my eyes jerked open at the sight of Orlov's knife coming towards me. My heart hammered as I jolted awake, and adrenaline pumped through me. I took a deep breath, then lay back as I realised I was safe. I felt Trent's arm around me, his hand spread across my stomach, tightening to hold me closer as if even in his sleep he'd felt me flinch. Turning over in the bed towards him I pressed my body up against his as he woke, responding to me as I knew he would, happy to give me whatever I needed because he loved me.

# Chapter 11

I slept late the next morning, my head still woozy and my body tired. Trent lay beside me, not long awake himself, asking nothing of me. We ate a lazy breakfast before showering and dressing. It was already late morning and I wanted to go and look at the horses, but on approaching the back door I found I didn't want to leave the cottage. Fear swept through me at the irrational thought that dangerous men could still be lingering on the estate.

"Trent" was my first word, unsteadily spoken. He was sitting at the table drinking his coffee, but he rose unquestioningly, threaded his fingers through mine and led me outside with Susie in tow. The horses had been put out to grass and, feeling safer having him with me, I went to the paddock to check on them. The hot sun blazed down on us, humidity levels already high. I let go of Trent and checked on each horse, though I was mostly concerned for Monty who was least able to cope mentally with the situation he'd been put in. He jumped slightly as I approached, and it was plain to see he'd lost weight drastically, his ribs showing clearly though he was grazing well, and I hoped he'd bounce back quickly. The others were fine and happy to greet me as I interrupted their grazing. I checked Regan's wound which had been cleaned and dusted with antiseptic powder. I was pleased to see it looked dry and already on the mend and he then stood patiently as I wrapped my arms around his neck and hugged him, breathing in the dusty horse smell I found so comforting.

I walked back to join Trent, surprised that he wanted to stay there rather than return to the cottage. I leant on the fence next to him and we surveyed the peaceful scene in front of us.

"I'm sorry, Em," he murmured rather awkwardly, not looking at me but at somewhere in the distance.

"Sorry for what?"

He hung his head, studying the ground in front of him, his foot scuffing a path through the longer grass. "For everything you've been put through."

"It was hardly your fault, Trent."

"I feel responsible, Em. All that talk about protecting you, but when it came to it I wasn't able to..." His voice tailed off.

"You couldn't be everywhere...your duty was to Cavendish. That's who was under threat."

"I can't help feeling I had my priorities wrong."

"You didn't Trent. You did what you had to do, and as I've told you before I don't need protecting." I said this in order to help him feel better, but it wasn't the truth. On this occasion I had needed him. I had needed him to protect me. I remembered how many times since our escape on the horses I'd wished he'd been there helping me, looking after me. Instead I'd spent that time not even knowing if he was still alive, believing my biggest fear had been realised. I'd been independent for so long it was hard for me to acknowledge, even to myself, this need for his protection, and now wasn't the time to mention it to him. I didn't want to make him feel any worse than he clearly already did. He didn't respond, but looked subdued as I continued, "You came for me, Trent, like you said you would. I couldn't have got through it without you," and then he smiled rather half-heartedly.

"I should have done better."

Returning to the cottage, we continued our recovery, resting and eating interspersed with brief conversation. Trent tentatively started to ask questions, drawing the information out of me as I answered him and asked my own questions in return, bringing each other up to date with what we'd been through.

Everything was comfortable until the evening when Trent took a call on a phone from his pocket. It was my phone, retrieved from the gravel where it had been thrown from the plane. His, I'd found out, had been destroyed by a bullet meant for him. I watched the transformation from calm to anger as he reacted to the call, swearing loudly at the messenger who I suspected was Cavendish. I was surprised; usually so calm and controlled it was so out of character. Still cursing, he ended the call, then realising I was listening tried to pretend nothing was wrong.

"Tell me," I insisted, and he came to sit next to me on the settee, taking my hand firmly. I guessed this was going to be bad.

"Orlov and the other two have escaped."

Fear flooded through me as I croaked, "How?"

"They were being transported between the police station where they were being interviewed and prison, and the convoy was intercepted. I knew they wouldn't take the threat seriously and be appropriately equipped. The result? Three policemen and two prison guards dead, and others wounded." Clearly frustrated, he leapt up and paced the room as he continued, "I told them of the dangers. I told them other gang members were on the loose and wouldn't leave them to be locked up. I told them, and they wouldn't listen. I even offered for our people to step in to take over. They would've been better prepared, better equipped for the situation, but the powers that be would have none of it. And this is the result, a bloody mess."

"Will they be coming here?" I asked, my anxiety rising. Trent took in the look on my face then came and knelt in front of me, his hands on my thighs as he tried to reassure me.

"No, of course not. They'll be out of the country by now – you don't need to worry about that." But I'd already pushed his hands away and gone to the back door to make sure it was locked. Susie followed me back into the room, watching me as I checked out of the front, currently paneless, windows, peering up and down the lane.

Trent called to me to come and sit down. He held me tightly, murmuring into my hair, "You're safe now, Em, no one's coming for you."

A short while later he disappeared out to the yard, and I watched him pacing and speaking furiously into the phone, making call after call until eventually he came in and collapsed on to the settee where I was trying, unsuccessfully, to read a book.

I looked at him, waiting for an update. He let out an exasperated sigh before giving me the gist of his calls. Following the attack on the convoy taking the men to prison there'd been no definite sighting of any members of the organisation in the country.

"That doesn't mean they've left, Trent."

"No, but they've been hit badly. They lost several people here and are going to need to regroup. Having lost the element of surprise they're not going to try this again soon...if at all," he added as an afterthought.

"So what happens now?"

"I've put a few calls out abroad, and obviously SIS are monitoring all intelligence that comes in. We should soon hear something regarding their whereabouts."

"And what do you think?"

"I think they will have gone to ground, getting back home as quickly as possible. Their mission was a failure and they will have been humiliated by their defeat. Orlov particularly," he finished, though he wasn't gloating.

Now was the moment to bring up something Orlov had said that had bothered me. Looking down at my book, I muttered, "He said you were just like him, that you behaved just like him. You're not like that, are you?" I couldn't believe it, but I didn't know what he got up to when on a mission, and I hated to think what he might have to do.

"No, Em, I'm not like him, not at all." I could hear the anger in his voice at the accusation. "I don't go around threatening women and children, using them as pawns like he does in his sick games. I take on the people who deserve it, the ringleaders, the ones who are in the wrong. Not the innocent. At some point, not now but at some point in the future, our paths will cross again, and he won't get away next time."

We kept to ourselves, and I was happy to only have his company. That was until the following day, when he said we'd been invited to the Manor for the evening. An informal get-together, was what he called it. I imagined something small and quiet, but later, as we approached the office, Trent stopped me and apologised.

"I'm sorry about this. I tried to stop them, but trying to stop Grace is like trying to hold back the sea. If it's too much we'll leave...okay? You let me know." And I was left wondering what I was letting myself in for.

Walking into the office felt like walking into an ambush. I knew Grace wouldn't have planned to make me feel awkward, but even so an uncomfortable hush descended as all those assembled turned towards us, no one quite sure how I would take the surprise. I could feel the frisson in the atmosphere and had the horrible feeling my arrival was that of an expected but rather disappointing guest; one that they were desperate to cheer or clap, or something equally embarrassing, but were having to hold themselves back.

Cavendish welcomed me warmly as Grace, breaking ranks, leapt forward and threw herself into my arms, to be joined by Sophia and Reuben. I was so pleased to see they

143

were all well and their exuberance was so infectious that I found myself smiling, and relaxed for the first time.

"Thank you, thank you, thank you," she whispered.

"You're welcome," I muttered, fighting back tears. When she eventually relinquished her hold on me I saw she was doing the same. Cavendish, bolstered by the smile on my face, turned to the room, raised his glass, and said, "To the best decision I ever made!"

Laughter broke out and the audience, taking it as their cue that I wasn't about to have a melt-down or bolt for the exit, started clapping, quietly at first but quickly building to a crescendo of claps, cheers and general whooping from the boys. Trent hugged me to him, grinning as I blushed horribly with embarrassment.

"Thank God that's over," he said as I exhaled with relief and Wade handed us a couple of beers. I was quite comfortable actually, now the awkwardness of our arrival was over. It was strange, but the experiences I'd been through, the fears I'd faced, had given me a renewed confidence in this crowd, as if I were one of them – no longer the outsider.

It looked as if this was to be a rerun of the meeting held only a few weeks before, though it felt much longer ago than that. Grace and Cavendish joined us at the drinks table as the noise level increased again. I noticed they held each other's hands, and wondered if, like us, they were feeling the need for that constant reassurance.

Cavendish said seriously, "I meant what I said, Grayson. I can't thank you enough for bringing my family back to me safely. I won't forget what you've done for us."

I could feel myself getting emotional again and wasn't sure why I found it so difficult to accept thanks. I tried to brush it off as being what anyone else would have done in the same situation, and thanked Cavendish for his kind words.

144

Mrs F arrived pushing a trolley which was loaded with huge pans of rice and chilli, and everyone dived in, eating, drinking and chatting. I looked around because there were a couple of people I particularly wanted to see. I spotted Porter by the fireplace and went over to him, interrupting as he was wolfing down his food.

"Hi, Porter," I mumbled, feeling guilty for being the reason he'd been shot, although mystified that he looked so well on it. "I wanted to say thank you for what you did for us, and...I'm really sorry for being the reason you got shot. I hadn't realised you had no backup at the farm."

"No reason why you should've known that, and certainly no need to thank me. I was happy to help out."

I couldn't understand why he was so casual about it. "Can I ask? How are you still alive?"

He guffawed with laughter, before replying, "It was thought that there was unlikely to be much action at the farm, so the rest of my support had been sent up to protect Cavendish at the Manor. When I got your call I knew I was going to be exposed opening the gate, so I put on my bulletproof vest and protective helmet, and gave you as much cover as I could to slow them down. I took a few shots to my broad and, though I say it myself, very manly chest, and fell to the ground as if I was on a West End stage, playing dead. They went straight past me in their eagerness to get after you, and I jumped up, brushed myself off and carried on with my evening."

His dramatic telling of the events, complete with actions, was very entertaining for those around him, but I marvelled at the fact that he told the story as if it were an everyday occurrence for him to be shot at. He added in a low voice, more seriously now, "Don't worry, Grayson, I've been in worse situations." I couldn't help admiring his nonchalance as I turned to Trent to ask where Turner was.

Trent frowned. "We've tried to get him in here, but he won't join us."

145

"Why not?"

"He's been very badly beaten, Em. He's not spoken much, but we think he feels he's let us down by getting taken hostage in the first place. He's embarrassed because Anatoly Polzin and his men made a fool of him in front of everyone, so he's shut himself away."

Trent and I hadn't talked much about the men that had come here, but I recognised the name and knew Anatoly was the youngest of the Polzin brothers. He had been one of the few, along with Orlov, who had been mentioned in the briefings before all of this had happened. Poor Turner. I hated to think how he must be feeling and said, "I want to go and see him."

"I'm not sure it'll do any good, you know."

"I have to at least try. He and I are the odd ones out in this place so maybe I can reach him. I can't bear to think of him on his own."

"Well I can see there's to be no stopping you, and it's good to see a little of your normal self coming back." He grinned. "I'll come with you because you don't know where he lives."

Turner shared a flat with some of the other boys. Trent produced the key he'd borrowed from Carlton on the way there, and once we were in the flat I knocked on the only door that was closed.

"Turner, it's me, Grayson. Can I come in?"

Silence.

"Turner, are you awake? I want to see you."

I heard movement from behind the door. "Grayson?" Turner's voice, groggy with sleep.

"Yeah, it's me, can I come in?" I listened to the silence. "Please?" More silence. "I'm not leaving until I've seen you, Turner."

Silence. Then when I'd started thinking I was going to have to come up with another tactic, I heard one word.

"Okay."

I pushed the door open. He was sitting on the bed facing me, staring at the floor. I was shocked at the state of him. He was hunched over and seemed to have shrunk. I sat down next to him. He flinched as I put my arm around his shoulders. Then I saw his face.

It was a mess of bloody contusions, violently coloured bruises, open wounds to his cheekbones and eyebrows. His lips were split and puffy. I dreaded to think what had been done to the rest of him. He kept his head lowered, as if ashamed by the damage that had been inflicted on him.

"Oh my God, Turner, what have they done to you?" I whispered as I reached out, placing my hand gently on his cheek. Then, most terrible of all, he lifted his face and opened his swollen, bloodshot eyes. I could see the raw pain inside, the tears on the verge of overflowing, but most worrying was the rage I could feel beneath it all; rage and a potent mix of hatred and fear. My tears came then as I held him to me, feeling his body racked with the release of his own. Over his shoulder I saw Trent turn away, then a murmur from the other room as he made a call. When Turner was calmer I sat back from him, then turned to look at Trent who had rejoined us.

"Has he had any treatment?"

"What I ordered him to have, but he accepted the bare minimum. He refused anything else. Stanton's on his way now."

Stanton and Lawson, or Mrs Stanton, or whatever she was choosing to call herself now, arrived within a couple of minutes, by which time I'd told Turner they were on the way to look after him, and as they got to work Trent and I waited in the sitting room.

Turner was eventually brought out of his room by Stanton, and though he didn't look much better, his cuts had been cleaned and dressed again, and Stanton told us he'd been dosed up on strong painkillers.

"Turner," I said, "we're having a gathering in the office which you need to be at. You're part of this estate and we need you there, even if it's only for a brief time."

"I can't go, I let everyone down." His head dropped again and I could feel his humiliation.

Trent said, "You haven't let anyone down, Turner, you were targeted. They took you because of your skills, but if you hadn't been there they would have found someone else to barter – someone else who was alone." He looked at me. "It could have been Emma. She was nearest to you in the woods, and she was separated from the others...it could have been her."

I swallowed, my throat suddenly dry. That hadn't even crossed my mind.

Trent continued, "We should have made sure that none of the pilots were isolated, Turner. I'm sorry we let you down."

"Will you come with us, Turner?" I asked. "You should be with your friends."

The briefest of nods, and I took his hand as I led him from the flat and we went back with Stanton and Lawson to the office.

The noise that rose to welcome Turner's entrance was enthusiastic. I hoped he wasn't going to find it too overwhelming. I stayed close to him while the first few came to greet him, then stood back as he was gradually drawn into the room, making his way to a seat where he remained for the evening surrounded by his friends, although he was quiet and withdrawn.

"I think we're going to have some difficulties ahead with him," Trent muttered.

It appeared that this meeting was being held as some sort of informal debrief. The children were sent to bed and we all settled down. With Sharpe making notes in the background, Cavendish outlined the set-up for the attack on us which unfortunately drew attention back to Turner, though Cavendish dwelt on this part as briefly as possible.

Everyone told their bit of the story as it went along, although there were regular interruptions for questions, additions and clarifications. Eventually it became clear that the attack on the Manor had merely been a diversion for the true goal – the kidnap of Grace and the children. The men who had taken Turner had seen that they were at the stables, so from then on everything had moved fast because while the family were divided it made it easier for the kidnap to take place.

Carlton and I then started on our part. I explained our escape on the horses, and remembering the man who had intercepted us I thanked whoever it was who had killed him. I looked round to see who was taking the credit, but saw only blank faces. I'd assumed the shot had come from someone on the roof of the Manor, but was told the distance was far too far for that level of accuracy. There was some pondering on this mystery, the consensus being that it must have been some sort of friendly fire incident, but that didn't rest easy with me. It hadn't felt like that; it had felt like an execution, but Cavendish concluded that the ballistics report would shed further light on to it when it came back, and we moved on.

The final part, but the bit which to me was the most important, was an update on the known whereabouts of the organisation's members. Cavendish had received a briefing prior to this gathering, and intel had been received proving Anatoly and Orlov were already back in their own country. As they were the leaders, it could be assumed the same applied to the rest of the gang. Trent whispered "I told you so" and I smiled in response.

It was late by the time we got to the end. I was exhausted, drained from the emotion of having to think about it all again, but pleased at the same time that I'd managed to get through it and it was over.

Though the security level remained heightened, the estate stood down from its high alert status, but this didn't make me feel any less anxious.

The week became hotter and more humid as it progressed, making sleeping difficult and the days sticky and uncomfortable. I didn't want to go riding yet. Well, I did want to ride; but I didn't want to be out on my own. I tried taking Regan into the arena, but couldn't concentrate. I jumped at every moving branch that caught the corner of my eye, every noise. Even the rock-steady fellow beneath me became twitchy, so I soon returned to the stables. Trent sauntered over from the cottage as I untacked.

"That didn't take long," he commented. I responded casually that Regan wasn't going right; obviously the horses needed some recovery time too. Trent didn't respond, but I felt his eyes following me.

I resumed the yard routine, thinking that one morning I would get up and find that my anxiety would have subsided, along with the queasiness I felt which I knew was brought on by the nervous energy running through me. When that morning came I knew I'd feel able to ride out again. Ironically my inability to do so only added to my anxiety levels.

At the end of the week I sat nibbling on my toast, edgy because the back door was open. It was nice to have what little fresh morning air there was in the current heatwave wafting through the door, but I still needed it to be closed. I rose. Trent reached out, placing a restraining hand on my wrist. "Leave it," he said. I sat, sighing as I pushed the rest of my toast away and picked up my tea instead, not sure I even wanted that. It had been like this all week: Trent opening doors, windows, encouraging me to eat in the garden; me closing and locking the same, and complaining the heat was too much to eat outside.

When my phone rang, I jumped. It was Carlton who, after asking how I was, casually said, "I thought I might go out for a ride today, wondered if you'd like to join me?" My eyes flicked to Trent's face as he took his time reading something trivial in the sports section of his paper.

"Don't you have something else you should be doing?" I knew full well that, although he enjoyed it, Carlton only rode when he had to.

"Nope, just kicking my heels, and the idea came to me."

Well of course it did. "I'm not sure, Carlton. I don't think they're ready to get back into exercise yet."

"Oh, come on!" he wheedled as he tried to win me round, and as if to entice me further he added "The first field has been harvested...", letting that temptation hang in the air between us.

Sighing deeply, and obviously, I replied with resignation, "Go on then."

"Excellent, I'll see you in ten." And he was gone.

"Not very subtle," I said across the table to Trent.

"What isn't?"

"You arranging for Carlton to ring me to go out riding."

"I don't know what you mean."

As I got up to go and get ready, I caught the briefest smile on his lips. It only served to irritate me more.

I'd tied the horses up outside, and as we tacked up I thought I should confront something I was still pretty ashamed about. I'd seen Carlton a couple of times since Trent had carried me down the steps of the plane, but it either hadn't been the right time or I hadn't been capable of talking to him. As I finished tightening Monty's girth I came out with it, not knowing how best to approach the subject.

"I'm sorry we left you the other night, Carlton. I feel terrible about it."

"It was the right decision," he replied in his typically offhand fashion.

"You didn't even question it?"

"Why would I? You made the right call. It's not as if there was a spare horse for me, and I bought you some time to get away, so don't stress about it."

I felt foolish worrying about things the people here seemed to take in their stride, but I still didn't like the thought of someone risking their life for me. It made me feel indebted.

Carlton only needed to take one look at me to realise how downcast I was, "Oh, don't look so miserable! Come here." And he hugged me, good and hard. "I'm still in one piece, Em," he said as he let me go, "that's all that matters."

I nodded and, moving to Monty's head to take off his headcollar, looked up to see Trent watching us from the garden.

Carlton was fortunately in one of his chatty moods, a good thing because I wasn't. I knew he was doing it to distract me from the route we were taking; to distract me from noticing the churned-up grass where wheels had spun in acceleration as they came for us up the lane only a few nights earlier; to distract me from the fact that we were riding on the exact same paths, leading in the exact same direction.

"Did we have to come this way?" I interrupted as I tried to calm Monty into walking in a normal manner instead of jogging sideways in an agitated state, caused, I knew, by my own unease.

"That's the direction the stubble field is in," said Carlton. I felt I would have happily forgone that particular thrill if I could have been heading the opposite way right now.

152

There was no one about as we went through the farmyard, and the gates stood open as if we were expected, and Carlton led the way through them and across the road. We'd warmed the horses up already, and as their feet touched the stubble Carlton was already geeing Regan up. "Race you!" He drove his heels into Regan's sides and, needing no excuse, Regan leapt forward.

In a futile attempt not to rise to the challenge I hesitated, holding Monty back, feeling his muscles bunching beneath me as his energy built. Realising resistance was useless, I relaxed my hands on the reins and leant forward in readiness as Monty exploded in hot pursuit of Regan. Carlton didn't stand a chance, but he already knew that. Within seconds we were coming up behind, then drawing level. I heard Carlton's whoop of joy, or encouragement; I didn't know which and it didn't matter. I was back where I needed to be, enjoying being in the moment and with adhrenaline pumping through me, feeling pure ecstasy. We galloped flat out, overtaking the others with ease, Monty's quality surpassing anything Regan could manage. The hot air cooled on our skin and I started laughing, loving the exhilaration and of feeling free. Slowly bringing Monty's speed down by doing a large circle at the end of the field, I came back up behind Carlton and fell into line with him again as we gradually calmed our snorting horses, before leaving the field and starting our walk back home.

Still smiling, I felt much better. The tension I'd suffered all week had been blown away. Leaning towards Carlton, I thanked him.

"No problem, Em, I wish I could cheer up everyone that easily." I knew he was talking about Turner.

"No improvement?"

"Physically he's getting better, the external wounds are healing up well, but it's the internal ones that everyone's worried about."

I'd heard this from Trent. He'd commented on how withdrawn Turner had become as he struggled with the humiliation of having been taken captive, how useless he'd felt at not being able to fight back, ending up being badly beaten before his captors had made him give them access to the estate. He didn't seem to realise that it would have been the same for anyone taken. Against those numbers, the odds were not in favour of the captive.

Trent had been encouraging him to talk to someone, to seek some sort of therapy in the form of a counsellor or psychologist, but Turner had so far proved unwilling, and Trent hadn't wanted to force the situation. "He'll go when he's ready," he'd told me, "there's no point in ordering him to go, he's got to want it too."

The horses had calmed by the time we returned to the yard, but were still sweating because of the heat, so granting Carlton his freedom for his good deed, I started to wash both of them down before putting them in their stables for the day.

As Carlton left Trent came out, holding the keys to his truck. He crossed the yard towards me and I looked up, flashing him a smile. I received one in return as he put his arms around me, seemingly oblivious as to how sweaty I was.

"You okay?" he asked.

"Much better, thanks, feels like I've blown off some steam."

"Been getting your heart racing again, have you?"

"Yes." I grinned, knowing he hated me taking, as he saw it, unnecessary risks.

"Hmm, I guess it's worth it...although I'm not too happy that it's another man that has put that smile on your face."

"If you could ride you would have been the one to put it there."

"Are you going to be all right if I go up to the Manor for a while? I've got a few things to do." I hesitated. He searched my face, then said, "I can stay...it's not a problem."

"No, no," I decided. "You go, it's about time you got back to work and stopped lazing around here. I'll be fine." I had to face this sooner rather than later, and while I was still on a high it would be better. He kissed me, but not for long enough, then left, and I finished off the horses before retreating to the cottage. I had to keep reminding myself to relax and not to keep checking around, not to keep glancing up into the trees or jumping at the slightest noise. Getting back to physical work was certainly a help.

It didn't mean I wasn't pleased when his truck returned as I was turning the horses out. Following him in I went to shower and prepare a salad for dinner. It was too hot for anything else. When we'd finished eating, Trent suggested going for a walk.

"It feels like it's going to rain. I've heard thunder rumbling around this afternoon."

"If we get wet, we get wet. At least it will be cooler. I don't want you starting to prowl around the house again like you have been doing."

"I don't prowl."

"Well pace then, up and down, up and down, checking the doors, the windows, the doors again."

I knew he was teasing, and he knew he was winding me up. "You're making me sound neurotic!" He raised his eyebrows at me.

I went to get my shoes on and we set off, Susie happily following but getting left behind when distracted by smells every now and then, scampering along to catch up. I could still hear the thunder and the sky had darkened, but we had gone well beyond the tree house before I felt the first fat drop of rain. I thought we might have been sheltered enough in the trees, but the rain that came was of the torrential type you get in summer when none has fallen for weeks and the land is crying out for moisture. Within a couple of minutes we were soaked. The fresh earthy scent rising from the woodland floor took me back to the tunnel, but not wanting that association I pushed the unwelcome thought away.

"We'd better turn back, find shelter under the tree house. Oh...wait a moment." And he bent down to retie his shoelace.

Sensing my opportunity, I called back "Race you" as I took off through the trees. I like to think I run like a gazelle; however, I know this is not so. Being slightly flat-footed, I've always found running a challenge. My current fitness level had improved things, but not by much, and the only chance I'd ever have of beating Trent would be by cheating. I could already hear him coming after me, and I'd seen him run. To watch him was to experience the joy of effortless and elegant beauty; he could eat up the miles with a graceful stride that seemed as easy to him as breathing. I'd never seen him doubled up in pain, gasping for air the way I did. That was what I was up against.

I ran flat out. I could hear him gaining on me, but as the tree house came into view I thought for one brief moment I might just make it. Then I felt his hands around my waist as he caught me. I squealed, then burst out laughing as he spun me dizzily around. Losing our balance we began to fall, and as Trent crashed to the ground he dragged me down with him, breaking my fall as I landed on top of him. Laughing as I tried to catch my breath, I could hear his deep chuckle as he pulled me up till my face was level with his. His hair was soaked, damp curls clinging to his forehead. Mine was just as wet. I ran my fingers through it, knowing it would be sticking up all over the place.

"You cheated," he stated, trying to reach my mouth.

"I thought you liked the chase," I challenged, knowing the truth, feeling the hunger in his kiss and eagerly responding. I thought for a moment I'd started something that might not be that easy to stop, but he suddenly let me go, breathing hard as he looked at me intensely. Then he smiled.

"Marry me?"

His eyes widened along with mine, as if these words had been as much a surprise to him as they were to me, but as my head was yelling "No" it seemed the most natural thing in the world for my heart to say "Yes".

# Chapter 12

At four-thirty the next morning, Trent found me sitting in a chair in the garden, wrapped in a blanket, Susie curled on my lap. He flopped down in the other chair before saying casually, "Wotcha doing?"

"Thought I'd watch the sun come up."

"Would've thought you'd done enough of that recently." A veiled reference to the previous week's events.

"I had other things on my mind at the time." I hesitated. "I think it's important to occasionally see the dawn, watch it come up, brand new day and everything..." I tailed off. As reasons went, it sounded contrived.

"So it's not that you can't sleep, then?"

"No."

"Or that you've got something on your mind?" I didn't answer, so he continued, "Talk to me, Em...what's going on?"

To be honest, I didn't know what was going on in my mind. I was confused. Only weeks before I'd feared losing him, made a ridiculous decision to leave which he'd managed to talk me out of, and now, having been through the worst and having him want to commit to me in such a final way, that didn't seem right either.

"It's this marriage thing." I paused, wondering how to avoid hurting his feelings. "Do you seriously think it's a good idea?"

"I wouldn't have asked if I didn't think it was."

"It's... it's just that we've both been stung by marriage before, and I was thinking that maybe we shouldn't go down that road again."

"You already said yes, Em. Are you wanting to take that back?"

"I don't know," I said. "We could live together, couldn't we? Isn't it a bit old fashioned...marriage?"

"I prefer the term traditional, and I am a traditionalist. It's important to me."

"What about all the things you'd be giving up?"

"Like what?" He sounded bemused.

"Like the apartment that you like so much and that suits you so well. I have to be here because of the horses. I can't live there, so you'd have to live here." He swept his hair back from his face with one hand as he replied.

"My home is wherever you are, Em. It doesn't matter to me what roof is over my head. Anyway, if you haven't noticed, I've already moved in."

I suddenly realised that of course he had. I couldn't remember a time when he'd chosen to sleep at his apartment when he didn't have to. Why couldn't I accept that he wanted me and be happy? Perhaps however far I moved forward I still felt as though I didn't deserve to find happiness. He carried on, his tone serious.

"Stop over-thinking this, Em. You and I need to be together, you know that. I like looking after you, when you let me, and I think you like looking after me. You can keep on putting up obstacles for as long as you like, but I will overcome each and every one. I am not Alex, I will not betray you or let you down...*and* you've already said yes, so unless you can come up with a valid reason for us not to get married" and standing, he held out his hand to me "I'm taking you back to bed."

I couldn't come up with anything else. His words did ease my worries and I wished I could be more like him. He was so confident, so definite, particularly where our future was concerned, and I knew he was carrying me along with him.

"I don't think I can go back to sleep now."

The sky was already lightening, a broken layer of purple-coloured cloud was tinged pink along its lower edge as the sun came ever closer to rising. Susie jumped down as Trent pulled me to my feet and took my hand to lead me in.

"I have no intention of letting you sleep."

"Are you going to tell everyone?" I asked as he ate breakfast and I toyed with a piece of toast.

"I thought we might go and see Cavendish and Grace later. Word will soon spread." He looked at me to see if I agreed with this course of action. I nodded. It seemed okay to me. He cleared his throat before continuing, "Before we see them, though, it might be a good idea to know what sort of wedding we want..."

"What were you thinking of then?" I asked cautiously.

"I'm not sure actually but do you want a church wedding? I have no idea if you're religious or not, but I'm happy to go for a church wedding if you are."

This was an issue for me. I used to go to church, I used to have a faith, but that had all gone when Eva died. I couldn't believe that the God who was supposed to love me could cause Eva to suffer and bring so much pain to me, and I'd turned my back on him. However, whenever I thought of Eva I couldn't imagine her as being anywhere other than in heaven, so it was complicated.

"No church," I replied.

"So I'd imagine there would be no problem with us getting married here then?"

"Sounds good."

"We could have something small, intimate..." I sensed he was testing out what I might be happy with.

"That would be fine. When were you thinking?"

He didn't even hesitate. "First weekend in September."

What? Was he insane? "This September?"

"Yes."

"As in the September that's happening in a few weeks' time?"

"Yes. Before the children go back to school. Why, what's the problem?"

"We couldn't get it all organised in time."

"What is there to organise? I'll sort out the paperwork, we invite everyone on the estate, they turn up and we say our vows. It couldn't be simpler..." Taking in the expression on my face, he stopped. "What's wrong?" I felt bad for not showing more enthusiasm, but I honestly didn't think that was entirely my fault. This time yesterday life had been trundling along again; I was only just getting used to being back to normal, and now suddenly I was under all sorts of pressure to organise a wedding – *and* for it all to be done within a very short space of time.

"There's more to it than that and you know it, and I don't feel up to organising it all at the moment, Trent. I still feel out of sorts after last week, and it all feels a bit overwhelming. There's food and music, and I'll have to get a dress..."

He stopped me. "I don't want you to be overdoing it, that's true. You do need time to recover. How about we talk to Grace and see what she might be able to help us with, and go from there? Knowing her, she'll want to take on the whole thing, and all you will need to do is get a dress."

Although she's meant to be recovering too, I thought. "One thing I would like in this simple wedding of ours."

"What's that?"

"No speeches."

"Works for me, although Cavendish may be disappointed. He'd love the opportunity to tell a few embarrassing stories about me."

"Ah, I hadn't thought about that, could be entertaining..."

Trent added quickly, "No, I agree with you, no speeches."

Cavendish and Grace were absolutely delighted when we told them later, immediately insisting that we held the whole thing there. Champagne was opened. Grace, brimming with excitement and ideas, soon excused herself and disappeared from the room. Cavendish watched her go, and I sensed his concern.

"Is she okay?" I asked tentatively.

"She will be, she will be," he replied brightly, repeating the phrase as if to convince himself. Then his usual enthusiasm returned as he poured more champagne. "This is just what she needs, actually, a project to get her teeth into, something else to focus on for a while. Organising a wedding will do her the world of good."

Whatever works for her, I thought. It certainly wasn't something I could cope with at the moment.

Cavendish knew his wife well. This news was exactly what she needed. Within half an hour it was as though the whole estate already knew, and if they weren't able to join us at the Manor then our phones rang with calls and texts of congratulation.

I felt out of my depth as the plans developed around me, Grace discussing the food and drink with Mrs F, then floating ideas past me. I nodded along to everything. I was sure whatever they came up with would be fine with me.

In the end the only thing I had to do was get a dress, and even that was felt to be too onerous a task for me to take on alone. On the following Monday, as soon as I'd finished the horses, I was picked up by Grace, Greene and Mrs F. We went to a wedding shop in the local town, and the others played dress-up using me as the doll. If the shop assistants found anything odd about my still blackened eye and the stitches in the slash across my arm, they made no comment, and neither did anyone else, although once I caught Grace staring at the wound, her eyes shining with barely-held-back emotion. I caught her eye and smiled, reassuring her it was okay. She smiled back shakily and turned away to look at veils, something that I did know was not going to be happening.

Once everyone else was happy with the choices made, and I apparently looked beautiful, which I thought unlikely, we returned home. I was content in the knowledge that I was going back to work properly the next day and would immerse myself in that.

That evening, as we ate dinner, Trent brought up the subject of whom to invite to the wedding. I thought we'd covered this. I thought we'd agreed to invite everyone on the estate, their other halves and families, which would come to a decent number. It wasn't as if either of us had family to invite. Trent had told me his parents had died only a few years ago, and he had no siblings or extended family. But he asked me if there was anyone off the estate that I wanted to invite. I looked over at him, searching his face for some clue as to why he would have brought this up. He knew my parents had died in a car accident when I was five. I'd been passed from one set of foster parents to another from then on until I'd met and married Alex straight from school. Surely he wasn't suggesting I invite Alex? Unsurprisingly, it turned out it wasn't Alex he was thinking of.

"I wondered if there was anyone from your past, possibly some of your foster parents, you might want to invite."

There wasn't. I'd only been fond of my first set, those who had taken me in when I was scared and alone, but my trust in them had been broken when, with no warning, I'd been sent to live with another set within a couple of years. It was then that I saw straight through them all. They were only doing this because they got paid to, and I never

163

allowed myself to grow attached to any of them again. I tried to explain this to Trent.

"So you never tried to stay in touch with any of them?"

I shrugged. "There was one exception. I remember when I had Eva, I suddenly had this need to get in touch with that first couple. Ben and Lisa. I had no one else to tell about my daughter, and I wanted to show her off to someone to show I was all grown up and how happy she'd made me. I went to find their house. I knew which village it was, though it was quite a way away, and once there I had to try and find their house from my memories. I did find it, only to discover they no longer lived there which was bitterly disappointing."

"So you didn't look any further?"

"I didn't bother because while I was there talking to the people who now owned the house, they were kind and called over a neighbour who had lived there thirty years or so, and though I didn't remember her she remembered me well enough. She remembered me leaving and how distraught I was. She was good friends with Lisa and had had to comfort her afterwards, she was so upset. But then that was that. The next day they were gone."

"Gone?"

"Yup, just like that apparently. No word to anyone, packed up overnight and left. No forwarding address, nothing. That's why the incident had stuck in her mind."

"That seems a bit odd."

"Yes...but it could have been any number of things, couldn't it? They were only renting so perhaps were in debt, behind with the rent, who knows? It would explain why they needed the money from fostering, but perhaps it wasn't enough. I reasoned that's why I was moved on." It was the only plausible explanation I'd been able to come up with, and Trent agreed it seemed reasonable.

"So there's no one else, then?" he reiterated. "I don't want you to regret not having invited someone at a later

164

date." I assured him there was no one else, and was happy to leave the subject.

Since my ride out with Carlton I felt more confident about going out on my own again, and assured Trent that I would be fine as I encouraged him back to work, practically shooing him out of the door. If he noticed whenever he returned home the door was always bolted, he didn't say anything. It was good to be back among the horses again, and when I rode out I rode hard and fast, keeping busy, active, my mind occupied.

I went back to working out each evening, hoping that the return to my previous routine would settle my body down again. I was often working out at the same time as Turner, and could see why Trent and the others were worried about him. He was always there when I turned up, and still there when I left. In fact, I gathered he was there until long after I left. He worked out hard and nonstop, keeping to himself and not letting up for a moment. I'd also seen him using the punch-bag, practising punches and kicks, so one day I wandered over when I'd finished and offered to hold the bag for him.

With barely a grunt he nodded, and I took up position. After a couple of kicks I tentatively offered some advice on improving his technique. He hadn't had any training, and I showed him how he could make his kicks more effective. He seemed to appreciate this, softening a little as he asked if he could hold the bag for me when I practised. This started to become a daily event, both of us working out, meeting at the end of my session for some punch-bag practice. Turner began to open up more, asking questions about the kickboxing I'd done. He was improving quickly. I was concerned he was pushing himself too fast too soon, but his wounds were healing well, and though his bruises were still visible they were fading. Sadly, though, an angry young man had replaced the light-hearted boy he'd been

165

before the beating. Turner appeared to be hellbent on building up, and I feared he was doing it to ensure he would be able to defend himself should there be a next time, determined never to be in that vulnerable a position again.

The days passed in a blur of activity, and the wedding plans fell into place thanks to those who were doing the organising. When I was needed, I popped into the Manor for Grace and the others to run things by me, and it was on one of those occasions that I bumped into Sophia and Reuben. I knew they'd been away for a week staying with some cousins, and because of that hadn't, in fact, been to the stables to ride since "the incident", which was how I now referred to it. I wasn't sure what else to call it.

I'd walked into the kitchen and there they were, perched on high stools up against the worktop, eating some sort of chocolate sundae, digging long-handled spoons into tall glasses of chocolate ice cream streaked with darker sauce. They turned when I entered, grinning which was good to see. They both appeared to have benefited from their week away, which I guessed was the plan, and looked healthy and bright-eyed. I would have loved to have had a little of whatever it was that was making them glow like that.

Plopping myself on to a stool next to them, but refusing the kind offers of a lick of their spoons, I was wondering if they'd heard the news and if I should broach the subject when Reuben jumped right in.

"Getting married then," he said, cramming another creamy mouthful in.

"Yes," I replied, a little taken aback at his abruptness. "How did you know?"

"Been asked to be best man...along with my Dad," he said indistinctly through the ice cream.

"Have you now?" That was news to me, though I liked the idea and the fact that Trent was including him. Then I frowned, saying, "Well now that's a shame – I was about to ask you to be a pageboy." I was winding him up and knew he wouldn't let me down. His expression turned to one of disgust at the thought.

"You don't fancy wearing some sort of frilly knickerbocker outfit, then?" I teased.

He shook his head, rolling his eyes at me. "No I don't, you'll have to find someone else for that job. I'm getting a suit to wear as best man."

I doubted they made suits durable enough to last a day without getting trashed by some of the stunts Reuben got up to. "Oh well," I sighed, "I guess I'll just have to manage without a pageboy then."

"What do they do then, at a wedding?" he asked.

I shrugged "Absolutely no idea" and he laughed. I turned my attention to Sophia who had been quietly eating throughout our exchange.

"Are you okay, Sophia?"

"Yes." But she wouldn't look at me preferring to concentrate on her ice cream instead.

I was suddenly concerned that maybe she didn't like the thought of Trent and I getting married. I knew how close she was to him and it made me feel uncomfortable, especially with what I wanted to speak to her about.

"Okay..." I thought I'd better ask. "Sophia, are you all right with Trent and I getting married?"

Her brief nod accompanied by a not-bothered lifting of the shoulders was not exactly the enthusiastic response I was hoping for, but I thought I'd plough on with my request.

"Oh, well...I was wondering if you would like to be my bridesmaid," I asked, not sure what reaction I was going to get.

She squealed as she leapt off her stool, scooted round to me and threw her arms round my neck, crying "Oh yes, yes please!" into my hair, before leaping back down, bouncing a couple of times and running from the room, yelling for her mother as she went. I was left with a lingering scent of chocolate and a sticky smear across my cheek.

"That seemed to make her happy," taken aback at such a turn-around in her mood.

"Yup...it's all she's been talking about: the wedding, the dress, would she get asked, what would her dress be like, what would she do if she didn't get asked, what would she wear then, and on, and on, and on..." Reuben said dramatically. I laughed and thought how easy it was to make a little girl's dreams come true. And, having made my first decision of the wedding, I thought I'd better go and find Grace to see if there was anything else I should be doing. At least she wouldn't have minded me having gone off script with this decision.


I was working out at the gym the following week and deep in thought. Whatever I did I couldn't shake off the uneasy feeling that at some point Orlov and the others were going to return, and with these thoughts and those of the wedding my mind buzzed with the overload. Physical work was good for giving me the head space to focus on these issues, but with my day job I was finding I had too much time to think, too much time to dwell on the endless possibilities of what might happen. Trent was keen for me to move on and wanted to put "the incident" behind us so I didn't want to keep bringing it up, but irrespective of my current problems, and I knew I was stronger now, the worries were mounting, and the more I thought about them the more I knew they needed confronting.

Though distracted by these concerns, at least all this activity was keeping my body in good shape, I thought. "*I can feel her body against mine, firm as I like it but soft in all the right places"*. I shuddered, pushing the memory back into the dark recesses of my mind, startled as I looked up to find Trent standing in front of the cross-trainer I was pounding, his arms crossed as he studied me. My thoughts interrupted, I came straight out with it.

"How do we know they're not going to come back – Orlov...and the others?" He didn't hesitate.

"We don't. In fact, if we do nothing it's inevitable that they will."

"What are we going to do then?" I fired back.

"Regardless of what happened here, we were given a job to do and we shall be redoubling our efforts with that after the wedding." This was news. He realised that from the look on my face as he continued, "Sorry, I probably should have told you that before." I ignored the apology – it wasn't unusual for him to keep stuff from me. At least now I knew some action was going to be taken, that we weren't going to sit here defensively – proactivity I could deal with – not that I liked the thought of him going, putting himself in danger. He frowned.

"We'll be keeping this place fully covered in our absence, Em," he said, as if trying to reassure. I was glad he didn't add "Just in case" and nodded, not slowing my pace.

He looked concerned as he asked, "Are you okay? You seem to be as intent as Turner on working out every moment there is. Sure you're not overdoing it?"

The truth was that I was overdoing it; my body was tired, but unable to shake the unsettled feeling that haunted me nowadays at least if I worked out hard I slept well. I wasn't sure why I was feeling like this all the time, but had put it down to being hypersensitive to everything around me, and the subsequent overactive adrenaline production was sending me into fight or flight mode too often and making me twitchy.

"I'm fine, Trent, a little out of sorts that's all."

"Hmm, I was wondering if you were up for a little sparring with Turner. I've watched you putting in some time with him, and if there's anyone getting through to him at the moment it's you. Thought it might do you both a little good...something different. What do you think?"

"Yeah, I'm up for that." I was willing to try anything to improve my frame of mind.

"Right. Well, to brief you, we're concerned that with all the work he's putting in he thinks he's better than he is, and we're worried he's going to take on more than he can handle. We need you to show him, as gently as you can, how much he doesn't know yet."

Oh, so it was not about trying something different, more about sending a message then, I thought.

"Okay," I said. "If you could get some mats out we can get ready." I called to Turner and suggested the sparring. Even without Trent's intervention it was about time Turner was exposed to the different discipline that was needed for this type of training, though it had been a while since I'd done anything like this and I hoped I wasn't too rusty.

I'd taken up kick-boxing a couple of years before coming to the estate. I'd found the exercise good for my mental health, and I'd frequently trained with sparring partners, ending up competing for my club a couple of times.

While Turner and I donned head guards, gloves and protective pads, the others laid out a square of mats. Then I introduced Turner to the art of defence and attack. We each tucked the ends of a shoelace into our waistbands, and the winner would be the first to snatch the other's shoelace. As well as learning about facing an opponent, keeping light on your feet ready to defend or attack, it was an exercise that taught the blocking skills needed to defend, which Turner had never learnt, and also taking on a live target in attack rather than an inanimate punch-bag.

It was, however, mostly about moving fast and blocking defensively, and it was frustrating for Turner: I did not go easy on him. It was his twentieth attempt before he had his first win, and by then he'd had to work seriously hard and definitely deserved it. He'd done well, learnt fast, but rather than take the well-deserved applause from our small audience, he handed me back my shoelace, checking his was still securely in position, then muttered, "Again." He turned his back to me and walked to his start position.

"Enough," I replied firmly to his back.

"I want to go again." He turned to face me.

"I said, that's enough...for today. Bring your game face for tomorrow though, Turner, because it's not going to be any easier." I grinned as I walked towards him, offering my gloved hands in as near a high five as can be done in gloves, and he reluctantly brought his hands to mine in salute. I knew we were done for the time being. I knew I was done for the day anyway, and wasn't sure I would be in any state for a rematch anytime soon, knowing all I was currently good for was going home to soak in a hot bath.

The next day I thought that now he'd learnt about facing an opponent we'd have a proper match to practise the attacking moves. Wearing body protectors this time, I set out the rules of engagement which are important in this type of arena. Less so when you're fighting for your life in a back alley somewhere, I imagined.

I was planning on using this as a coaching session – stopping and starting to emphasise good and bad technique, the idea being not to kick the crap out of each other, but to do reined-back versions of the moves so that we would both still be standing at the end. Turner was young, fit and keen, and although I was worried about his desire for achievement at the moment, I felt that most importantly he wanted to learn.

The gym was empty, the boys having been called to the Manor to help Grace out. We started off easily enough, joking and laughing if the other miskicked, encouraging and congratulating each other if a blow landed satisfactorily. I knew Turner was holding back, though, knew he could do better and, driven as he was, I wanted him to work harder. I started attacking more aggressively, making him have to defend as I pushed him, hoping he'd start attacking back. The atmosphere changed between us as I laid it on, wanting him to come back at me, wanting him to put up the fight I knew he had in him.

"Come on, Turner, you can do better than this," I pushed as my foot collided with his comfortably padded ribs, receiving barely a grunt in response. Backing off again, I bounced on my toes, expecting him to retaliate and come for me. Nothing.

"You're overthinking this, Turner. Come on, here I am, an open target. Come and show me what you've got Turner." Goading now, I wound him up as he took on an attacking stance, primed, ready to go. I didn't let up. "Imagine I'm the enemy, Turner, imagine your worst enemy standing right here in front of you. Standing here open and waiting for you – what would you want to do to him if he were here now Turner? If Anatoly were here now..."

Big mistake. At the mention of Anatoly's name, Turner's fury erupted. I could almost see the red mist descend as he let out a primeval roar and unleashed a full attack on me.

Crap, what the fuck had I been thinking? As he launched himself across the mats at me, the realisation dawned that the gym was empty and Turner was about to kill me. I moved quickly, ducking and blocking as well as I could against the blows that rained down on me. I could do nothing other than defend, the blows coming too quickly to let me retaliate. I did the best I could, but

172

realised I was no match for his strength now that it was at full force.

A movement in the corner of my eye. The door opening, distracting me for a fractional moment. All that was needed. His foot catching me hard under my chin, throwing me into the air. I heard Trent's yell as I flew backwards, landing hard on the corner of the mats, skidding off and coming to rest against the base of the cross-trainer. Winded, I struggled to rise, needing to see where my opponent was. I knew he would be coming for me again, and I couldn't protect myself on the floor. Trent reached me, shielding me as he grabbed me to him protectively. Over his shoulder I saw Hayes and Carlton take hold of Turner. They took him down, pinning him to the floor until he was calmer, until all we could hear were his sobs of frustration and pain.

Struggling out of Trent's arms, I crawled across the mat to Turner as the boys began to loosen their hold. I knew the fight had gone out of him, and I put my arms around him, holding him tight as he cried "Sorry, sorry, sorry" over and over into my neck until it was wet with his tears.

Eventually he calmed enough for me to let him go, and we both sat silent and shocked on the mats. Taking my headguard off, feeling the tenderness along my jawline with my fingers I heard Trent behind me.

"What the hell happened?"

"It was my fault," I muttered, embarrassed at what I'd done, "I wanted him to do better, I pushed him, I goaded him." And looking up, I met the pain in Turner's eyes.

"What were you thinking?" Trent cried. "He could have killed you."

"I know." My voice rose. "I wanted him to bring his best and...he wasn't...so I..." I gave up my feeble attempt at explanation.

Trent sat for a moment pensively, his arms encircling his knees. He said to Turner, "We need to get you some

173

help. You do see that now, don't you? We can't risk something like this happening again if you lose it. I'll have a word at the station, see what they've got set up there that we could tap into."

Turner nodded mutely. I held out my hand to him and said, "I'm so sorry" before helping him to his feet. Stripping off the rest of our protective gear, we left the gym, all dejected by the way things had turned sour so quickly.

The next day Trent returned from the Manor carrying a huge bouquet of flowers, which was a first.

"Thank you," I murmured, a little mystified at what I'd done to deserve these.

"They're not from me," he explained, "they're from your new admirer." Then, seeing my raised eyebrows, he added, "Turner. Seems he feels the need to keep saying sorry to you because you made him nearly beat you to death."

"That's a bit of an exaggeration," I replied uncomfortably.

"Oh, you think so? It was just as well we walked back in when we did, wasn't it?"

"I'm sorry you're annoyed with me, Trent."

I heard the frustration in his voice as he said, "You make it so damned difficult to look after you, you know that?" Pulling me into his arms he held me close.

"I've told you before, I don't need looking after." He didn't respond to that directly; he knew I had needed him, he knew he had protected me from Turner and things could have turned out very badly if he hadn't. But he didn't rub it in.

"Humour me, will you? It's what I need to do."

# Chapter 13

Our wedding day, "the big day" as we'd come to refer to it, had arrived, and apart from my stomach that felt as though it was filled with butterflies, and my bruised jaw from Turners kick, that was now only uncomfortable if I talked, ate or moved it, I felt good. Buoyant even. It had been strange to wake up on my own that morning as Trent, being the traditionalist he was, had insisted we should spend our last night apart. He had returned to his apartment only to find his proposed quiet night in invaded by the boys and Cavendish, who'd decided to have an impromptu stag night. I imagined there'd be a few sore heads this morning, and from the slurred phone conversation I'd had with Trent in the early hours I hoped his wasn't one of them.

Trent had left the night before in his new, though temporary, toy. There wasn't much for me to do towards the wedding arrangements, so as a little gift for Trent, and with Cavendish's help, I'd hired a classic convertible Jaguar for a few days as a surprise for him. It had been delivered the previous day, when the first I'd known of it had been the roar of the engine as it approached the stables when he came to show me. It was deep red, and I had to admit he did look good in it. Since then there'd barely been time for the engine to go cold. Laps had been taken round and round the estate, Trent feeling the need to take everyone out for a ride as he enjoyed every moment racing it around irresponsibly. It was good to see him so happy and to know I'd played a part in that, both short term and, I was hoping, the longer term.

I got the horses ridden early and, now the heatwave was over, turned them out in the field and prepared the stables ready for the evening, when someone else would be coming to put them away. I went back to the cottage, and knowing Grace, Sophia and Greene would be arriving soon so we could get ready together, I went up to shower and wash my hair, hearing them noisy in the kitchen as I turned off my hair dryer. I joined them downstairs and opened the day's first bottle of champagne, with lemonade and just a splash of the bubbles for Sophia, and we raised our glasses to each other as my nerves kicked up a notch with the realisation that this was actually happening. I didn't know why I was nervous. I knew Trent and I were right together, I had no doubts there. But then I'd known Alex and I were right together too, and look how that had turned out. We chatted while I got out the smoked salmon nibbles I'd made to help soak up the alcohol, then we started to get ready.

Grace had brought my bouquet with her, containing only lily of the valley, simple and small. Greene did my makeup and hair, then it was time for the dresses. Greene and Grace had become my unofficial people for this event, but none of us wanted them to look like bridesmaids so they'd bought different dresses in complementary colours. Greenes' was of deepest burgundy for the garnets I wore in my ears and at my throat. Grace's was midnight blue and Sophia's silvery white, sparkling and glittering with tiny crystals, the pair of them matching the sapphires and diamonds that alternated around the plain band of white gold that Trent was going to put on my finger today. He'd already tried to give me the ring, left to him by his mother, shortly after asking me, but it was so beautiful and meant so much to him I'd wanted to save it for my wedding ring.

Joining me upstairs, Greene helped me into my dress, smiling with satisfaction as she looked me up and down, clearly pleased with the job she'd done. Then she turned me around and allowed me to look at myself in the mirror. My eyes widened in surprise at the vision before me, and I met her smile as she looked over my shoulder. My dress was ivory, soft folds sweeping across my breasts, the material reaching up and over my shoulders where it was held at their widest point, elegantly leaving my shoulders and neck bare, and then fitting like a comfortable second skin it dropped to the floor, so I could just see the toes of my shoes. A small pool of material flowed on to the floor behind me like cream poured from a jug as I turned to see more soft sculpted folds mimicking those across my chest but lying lower on my back.

I'd wondered if I'd needed to get such a dress. When I'd married Alex we hadn't bothered. Young and impetuous, we'd barely even told his family, knowing they'd disapprove of me, and I'd had no one to tell, other than Amy, before arriving at the registry office in our best clothes but nothing special. It had seemed rebellious at the time; reckless, though still right.

This time it was different; this time it was special. Having both been through so much to even get to this point, finding each other had been like a miracle, and we were now surrounded and supported by a family that felt closer to us than ours ever could be. It was an occasion that called for a dress such as this; even I believed I looked good.

"Thank you, Clare," I murmured, unable to tear my eyes away from the mirror.

"No crying, you're not ruining my artwork." She frowned, and I blinked vigorously, smiling away the gathering tears as I turned to her.

"Could you give me a minute?"

"Of course, but the car will be here soon."

She left the room and I took a deep breath, letting it out slowly as I wrapped my hands around the ironwork at the foot of the bed. Glancing over at my bedside table, I looked at Eva as she gazed back at me, wondering what she would have made of all this, briefly imagining her in the dress that Sophia was wearing, sparkling and glittering with tiny crystals, my angel. I'd imagined her here today as my bridesmaid before realising that, of course, that would never have happened. If she were still here, Alex and I would no doubt still be together, a happy family. Then I smiled at the thought of what her reaction would have been on being presented with such a dress, seeing her arms crossing, her scowl. She'd have dug in her heels at any attempt to make her wear such an outfit. I tore my eyes away from her before I became maudlin.

Attempting to make a grand entrance into my kitchen, I was delighted to see Sophia's eyes widen when she saw me. "You look like a princess!"

"Not half as much as you do," I replied as she spun in a circle to show herself off, giggling. Looking at the others I had to admit we made a handsome group.

Grace went to the back door as we heard a car pull in. Looking back at me, she said, "Wade is here with our lift, are you all right for us to go? We can hang on if you like, for a bit longer...Carlton will be here for you soon."

"You go...I'll be fine. You all look fabulous. Thank you." I was smiling, but my voice was shaky, my lip a little wobbly, and I could feel the tears building again. I wanted to let them know how much they meant to me – so much, but I knew I wouldn't get through it with words. I hoped my hugs would convey all that I wanted them to.

With a final warning from Greene not to cry they left, laughing and giggling down the path as Wade helped each of them into their seats and they set off, waving furiously at me.

Going back into the house I took a few deep breaths and started pacing, not fast, just steady, up and down, up and down, across the kitchen into the living room to the front wall of the cottage, before turning and pacing to the back door, then repeating. Susie watched me in that cool, steady way of hers, so devoted to me that she accepted whatever I did, however weird I might appear to her, both of us knowing that as long as we were together we would be all right.

I turned at the front wall to start my return journey to the kitchen, and stopped, abruptly. Carlton stood at the back door, silhouetted in the frame, his features becoming clearer as he moved towards me. I hadn't heard his approach, so deep had I been in my thoughts. He held his hands out and took mine in his as he reached me. He gazed at me, and I tried not to feel self-conscious. I was clearly going to have to get used to this kind of attention today.

"You look...stunning," he murmured, and then he surprised me by leaning forward and kissing me gently on my lips. He stood away from me and let go of my hands as he held his up as if in defence. "I promise that is the first, last and only time that will ever happen. Sorry, but I couldn't let today pass and know I'd missed the chance of ever doing that." He grinned awkwardly, a little embarrassed as he waited for my reaction, which was slow in coming but actually I felt surprisingly all right about it.

"That was...unexpected...but very sweet, Carlton. Thank you – as long as it's a one-off," I warned gently, then checked his watch as I wasn't wearing one. "We'd better go."

I bent to stroke Susie, scrabbling her ears in the way she liked, then, taking Carlton's arm, went out the back door.

As we walked down the path, Carlton asked quietly, "Are you...er, going to tell Trent...about, you know, me kissing you back then?"

"Of course not. What's to tell? It was a gesture between friends, wasn't it?"

"Thank you," he said, smiling over at me. It was good being this comfortable with him.

The car was Trent's loaned Jaguar and not the easiest thing to get into, even with Carlton's help. Managing not to shut my dress in the door, Carlton leapt into his side and, back to his usual ebullient self, set off, engine roaring as we approached the Manor. I was glad I had short, easily managed hair and not some fancy styled affair that would by now look like I'd been pulled through a hedge backwards. We pulled up in front of the door which opened immediately, and Carlton ushered me into the hall to join Grace, Greene and Sophia. I was checked over, probably for bits of dead fly stuck to me, and my hair was smoothed as Greene growled at Carlton for delivering me in this condition. I wasn't listening. Behind the double doors that led to the drawing room I could hear a low, level hum of whispered conversation. I stared at the doors, knowing I was going to have to walk out in front of all those people, knowing that they would all be staring.

This day had come so quickly I'd barely had time to think about it, so crowded was my head with afterthoughts of "the incident". That had probably been Trent's plan, I thought a little uncharitably. My initial concerns hadn't exactly gone away, more been drowned out, and though I'd faced my fair share of fears over the last few weeks, here was another waiting to test me. And now I was here, I wasn't sure I'd given this one enough thought.

Greene stood back and I knew we were ready. Carlton was going to go ahead with Grace and Greene. Sophia was going to stay with me and follow me in; she had told me that was the correct thing for a bridesmaid to do, and who was I to deny her? She carried a matching, though smaller, bouquet to mine, and stood ready for her big moment as I mustered all the courage I could for what I had to do, and tried to relax and smile at her. I could feel my heart beating fast as I slowed my breathing, remembering Trent's words *"Control your breathing and you will control your fear*", and I realised everyone was looking at me anxiously.

Grace put her hand on my arm. "Are you sure you want to do this alone, Emma? One of us could walk in with you...Carlton could..."

I shook my head. I was alone; that was the point, wasn't it? I told them to go, join the others, before my nerves got the better of me and I changed my mind. Carlton opened the door wide enough to allow them all to pass through then, giving me one of his grins, they were gone. The door closed.

With Sophia behind me I stood in front of the doors. I heard music start up. The noise level dropped and my heart pounded in my chest. I was alone. This was how it should be, with no one to give me away. I was alone, but after this I wouldn't be again – and that was a good thing – wasn't it? I knew his level of commitment, his need to be bound to me, and I wanted that too...didn't I? Doubt crept in, along with my growing desire to run from those doors and the crowd behind them.

And then the handles turned and the doors opened. I saw only him, his eyes, the crowd melting away until it was just him. I took a step forward.

Standing at the far end of the room, he looked confident as always, drawing me towards him with that smile of his. I felt myself relax, my breathing calm, and when I reached him our lips met, soft and gentle, safe at last. A giggle came from behind, a murmur, a polite cough to our side with the whispered words "I think you might have jumped ahead". A ripple of laughter made its way to us as we pulled apart, grinning through our embarrassment. Pausing to give an apology to the registrar, who was smiling, I turned, trying not to meet anyone's eyes. Feeling a little flustered I handed my bouquet to Sophia who, proudly carrying it before her, went to sit next to Grace.

I turned back towards the registrar. Trent took my hand in his and asked quietly, "Are you okay?" I nodded, took a deep breath and, letting it out slowly, tried to appear a little more composed.

We'd met the registrar before. Her name was Maggie Kean; she wore a dark green suit that fitted snugly around her ample curves; her hair, which appeared to have been frozen in place, was blonde, but not naturally; she was probably in her late forties and she giggled a lot. I'd noticed this when we'd met. Trent hadn't, or said he hadn't. Maggie giggled at everything he said, and I suspected that she was more than a little bit taken with him. The most interesting part of the meeting, though, was the point when I'd found out what Trent's first name was. He'd had the ridiculous notion of keeping it as a surprise for the big day, but when I'd pointed out that it wouldn't look great if I burst out laughing on the big day he'd looked hurt, grumpily telling me it wasn't that funny a name. Let me be the judge of that, I'd responded, and I was now hoping that it didn't cause any sort of reaction in the room.

Maggie was wearing glasses, and made a point of looking sternly at us over the top of them as if to warn us against stepping out of line again. Then, smiling warmly, she began.

"I am delighted to join all of you here at Melton Manor, which has been duly sanctioned according to law for the celebration of marriages, to join together Ezekiel Trent and Emma Grayson."

I met Trent's eyes and he smiled back, though his eyes then narrowed at the smattering of noise that broke out behind us. A stifled guffaw that I was sure was Carlton's. Trent's jaw clenched, but he gave no further indication that he had noticed as silence resumed and Maggie continued.

"If any person present knows of any lawful impediment to this marriage they should declare it now." Silence. Maggie paused for a long moment as if she willed someone somewhere to leap up and halt the proceedings, but the silence remained.

"Before you are joined in matrimony I have to remind you of the solemn and binding character of the vows of marriage. Marriage, according to the law of this country, is the union of one man with one woman, voluntarily entered into for life to the exclusion of all others."

Concentrating on Trent, she asked, "Are you, Ezekiel, free lawfully to marry Emma?"

"I am."

Then changing her attention to me, she smiled reassuringly. "Are you, Emma, free lawfully to marry Ezekiel?"

"I am."

Maggie looked back to Trent, encouraging him in his next words with the merest raising of her eyebrows. Her head bobbed, though not a hair moved out of place. He turned to me, taking my hands in his.

"I call upon these persons here present to witness that I, Ezekiel Trent, do take thee, Emma Grayson, to be my lawful wedded wife. For the privilege of having you take me as your husband, Emma, I promise to love, cherish and protect you, when you allow me to" and he grinned, "to encourage and support you in everything you want to do, and to be open and honest with you, as long as we both shall live."

I swallowed, my mouth suddenly dry. My turn had come. Maggie gently prompted me again, and I spoke.

"I call upon these persons here present to witness that I, Emma Grayson, do take thee, Ezekiel Trent, to be my lawful wedded husband. I have chosen you to spend my life with, Trent. I promise to care for you and to cherish you and to be loyal, loving and true to you as long as we both shall live."

Letting one of my hands go, Trent turned away slightly and I saw Cavendish and Reuben standing behind him. Reuben was patting down his suit in a dramatic display of searching for something, and right at the point when I could feel Trent's patience reaching its limit he fished into his breast pocket and his fingers came out, the ring brandished with a flourish, much to the enjoyment of those around us. Trent took it from him and slid it on to my finger.

"I give you this ring as a token of my love and a symbol of our future together."

Maggie beamed at us both before pronouncing us husband and wife, adding, "And *now* it is time for the kiss." And his lips met mine amid a crescendo of applause and laughter swelling around us, then separating he held my gaze, his eyes warm, glowing and triumphant as, both smiling, we turned to our audience which was on its feet.

As the room settled we had a brief moment before we were called over to sign the register. The room was buzzing with hushed conversations, and I took the opportunity to look at Trent in a way I hadn't managed on first entering the room. In his impeccable charcoal-grey suit, crisp white shirt and silver-grey tie he looked gloriously handsome, and leaning in to him, I murmured, "You scrub up well."

His hand, already in the small of my back, pulled me closer, his other tipping my chin up to his face as he replied, "Not half as well as you do." His lips brushed mine, and he paused before adding, "You look beautiful, Mrs Trent." And the way he looked at me made me feel it.

# Chapter 14

Once all the formalities were over we led the way back down the aisle, confetti showering down on us, and headed to the ballroom where the celebrations were to continue, as informally as possible, we hoped. Caterers had been brought in so everyone on the estate was able to celebrate with us, and they were ready with champagne and canapés as we were hugged and kissed by all while classical music played softly in the background.

There were other children around of all ages, so Sophia and Reuben had company, and there were so many more people to meet. There had been an open invitation to everyone, their families, partners, girlfriends and boyfriends, and all had come. Once the drink was flowing and the conversation and laughter was rising in volume, we took the opportunity to wander out through the doors that stood open, leaving the terrace and taking to the grass as we walked round the garden, our fingers laced together, happy in the silence and peace between us.

At the far end of the garden, and alone for the first time, Trent turned to me, pulling me close as he kissed me longingly. Making me wish we didn't have to return to the party. The moment was broken as a group of shrieking children ran past us with Reuben and another boy, Porter's son James, brandishing water guns, more like cannons from the size of them, in hot pursuit. We looked over to the direction they'd come from to see Hayes and Wade laughing, and suspected that they'd instigated the interruption. Laughing, we walked slowly back to join the party now spilling out of the ballroom.

Dinner was relaxed and sumptuous. A few glasses were raised in toasts, but no speeches, as promised. The band started to warm up and Trent and I separated, mingling and chatting with our friends, but every now and then I found myself looking up, seeking him out, and as if I'd physically touched him his gaze would come to meet mine. I was reminded of the barbecue we'd attended here only a few months ago on the evening before our first night together. So much had happened since, so much that had threatened to change us, yet here we were and nothing had changed at all.

The band began to play, and as dancers took to the floor Trent made his way back, a glass of wine in each hand as he sat on the chair next to me.

"You okay?" He handed me a glass.

"Absolutely fine, thank you, it's been great, Trent. Thanks for arranging all of this."

"I can't take the credit for it all, you know that." From the toast he'd made, thanking everyone who had been involved, I did know how much help he'd had, but still I wanted him to know I didn't take it for granted.

He took a sip of wine, putting the glass gently down on the table before turning to me. "It's nearly time for our first dance together as husband and wife."

"You're joking?" My eyes widened in disbelief at what he was suggesting, remembering back to our first dance together at the May Ball. Neither of us being able to dance, we'd shuffled round in a circle, and I thought that sort of display was hardly something to show off in front of everyone.

He was smiling his confident, knowing smile. Suddenly it clicked into place. "Ah..." I said slowly, "you can dance."

"Of course."

"So why did you say you couldn't?"

"We didn't know each other so well then and it suited my purpose at the time, which was to be able to hold you as close to me as I could. However, I have made vows to you today to be open and honest, so I'm coming clean...also I wanted to give you a few surprises." He grinned, looking very pleased with himself, which was infuriating.

"It makes no difference, I still can't dance."

"Oh...come on, Em, we know each other better now. We know how each other moves, how we fit together." His words were soothing and seductive. "You'll find you're better than you think you are." Taking my hand, he pulled me up into a standing position, placing his hand firmly in the small of my back so I could feel its heat as he started towards the dance floor. "And anyway, I'm a great lead." I saw him nod to the band, who swiftly started to reorganise themselves ready for us. This had clearly been carefully planned and I didn't want to let him down, but my legs quaked beneath me and I felt sick at the thought of showing him up in front of everyone.

"Who says?" I responded sharply, wondering which fleet-footed vixen had boosted his ego with this praise.

"Cavendish."

"*What*?"

"All boys' school, Em, I told you that. Our foxtrot was something to behold!" He flashed his eyes at me, laughing at my expression. I couldn't get rid of the image that had now been implanted in my mind.

Our guests had cleared the floor, and now gathered round to watch. My legs were turning to rubber as Trent brought my arms up and into the correct position.

I muttered, "I'm not sure I can do this." Panicked thoughts of tripping, falling, taking him down with me, flitted through my mind.

"'Course you can. Anyway you're not going to have a choice, and you'd better brace yourself because I'm taking

187

you with me." His leg pushed against mine, forcing me to step back, and we were off. The music was modern. I recognised it as something Trent had been playing frequently recently, and now I knew why. I could feel my tension building, stiffening across my shoulders. I gripped his hand tightly.

"Relax, Em, I've got you," he murmured, and he really had. I was swept across the floor, releasing the breath I'd been holding, feeling myself relax as I did, my hand unclenching from his then tightening again as we reached a corner. He negotiated me round it. Clapping and cheers surrounded us; I couldn't believe we were actually doing it. I got the hang of the steps, and as long as Trent wasn't about to throw me a curve-ball in the shape of anything more adventurous I felt I could get through this without making a spectacle of myself.

Then the pressure was off. Others joined us on the floor. Trent's previous dancing partner, Cavendish, and Grace came past us, looking considerably more accomplished. And once the floor became busier it was just us two again and we slowed down, moved closer, Trent meeting my eyes, and as always when we were this close the intensity grew. His hand moved to my face, cupping my jaw, his fingers in my hair as his lips touched mine, dancing and kissing, kissing and dancing, as we spun round the floor. As the music ended Trent held me tight, then led me back to my safe area among the tables where I was considerably more at ease.

"Can't believe I did that without falling over."

"Told you I was good..." He chuckled as I raised an astonished eyebrow at his lack of modesty.

"At least there's nothing wrong with your ego. Go and make yourself useful, husband, by getting me a drink, please..."

"Of course, Mrs Trent." And kissing my hand, he walked away. Hmm...I was going to have to do something about that. Mrs Trent was not going to work, and I didn't think he was going to like it. I watched him cross the room, intercepted by Cavendish with whom he exchanged a brief word which looked strangely serious in the circumstances. Then they beckoned Wade and Hayes over to them, and all continued casually towards the bar but looked anything but casual to me.

I had meant to go over to chat to Bray and Mrs F, but instead I headed to the bar, stopping short at a table where Burton and Young were seated, deep in conversation. Then, seeing Greene and Carlton enter the ballroom, I waved Greene over to join us while Carlton made his way to join the others at the bar.

"What's going on?" Greene queried, then, looking at me, added, "Are you all right?"

"I'm fine, just need a bit of cover," I said in a low voice, surreptitiously inclining my head towards the bar. "They're up to something, I can feel it. Look like we're deep in conversation while I try and listen." Greene's eyes flicked to the bar then back to me.

"It might be them organising a surprise for you. It is your wedding day," she whispered as I tried to tune into the conversation behind me. I could hear only snatches.

"More surprises? Didn't you see me dance? That's more than enough for one day. No, it's something else." I heard the words "'ballistics report'". It sounded as though Cavendish was filling the others in; presumably the report had arrived. I could only pick out the odd word or phrase: "calibres", "casings", "checked against known firearms".

"Now that Trent has gone all open and honest with you, why don't you just ask him later?"

I rolled my eyes at Greene's naïvety.

"Matching     firing     pin     markings...breech markings...striations."

"Trent likes to protect me, he knows I've struggled getting over "the incident". I don't think this is something he'll be sharing." I heard "one anomaly...the man at the stables", and Carlton's voice asking, "What does that mean?" Good question.

"Trent's spotted you, he's coming over," muttered Greene, then she laughed as if I'd made a joke. Trent arrived at my side, handing me my wine.

"Sorry to keep you waiting, we got talking."

"Oh...what about?" I asked, gulping a large mouthful of wine. Greene took her glass from Carlton as he joined us.

"The ballistics report is back, and Cavendish was giving us the highlights."

"Anything interesting?"

"In what?"

"The highlights."

"No, much as expected." He shrugged as if to emphasise just how unimportant it all was. Hmmm, I thought, catching Greene's eye. "I'm going to get some cheese, do you want some?"

"No, but I think Carlton does. I'll come over with you. You coming, Greene?"

We followed our men in their search for more food. There was a table with a selection of cheeses and a variety of crackers, and anything you could possibly want to go with them in the way of chutneys and fruit.

Carlton pulled up seats next to us for him and Greene. Leaning across, he raised a glass to us, and I was suddenly aware how much he'd been drinking as he turned to Trent and said, grinning, "So, do we get to call you Ezekiel from now on – or do you prefer Zeke?"

Trent scowled. "I think it's probably safest for you, Carlton, if you stick to Trent."

I thought back to the conversation we'd had about why he'd stopped using his first name. It was when we were on our way back from the registrar's office, and he'd told me he'd hated his name when he was young. He'd thought Ezekiel Trent made him sound like a character out of a

Dickens novel, and he'd got teased mercilessly at a school where he was surrounded by those with safe, traditional names like Charles, Henry and George. From then on he'd dropped the name, and anyone who mentioned it. It was a shame. I thought it was beautiful.

Trent turned to Carlton now and said, "Of course, you will have to call Emma by her new name."

Carlton finished his mouthful of cheese, then, shaking his head, he said, "Oh I don't think so. If we stick with tradition here, Mrs T just isn't going to work. Makes her sound like an extra from The A Team."

Trent glared at him and laughter broke out around us. I tried not to join in, but couldn't help smiling broadly until Trent eventually succumbed along with the rest. "Okay...okay," he sighed, conceeding with resignation, "guess it will have to stay as Grayson then."

Our group began to expand. Tables were pulled together as more people joined us and others came and went, dancing, drinking, chatting. Some of the younger children, exhausted but refusing to admit it, flitted back and forth, torn between the lure of the older ones and the dance floor and the comfortable laps of their parents. Once the port came out and started circulating it looked as if we were set in for the night. The band eventually finished and joined us, and music was left playing softly in the background.

I'd had enough to drink, having passed on the port, and was relaxed as I watched the children play, not realising how transfixed I was by them until I felt Trent squeezing my hand. It clearly hadn't been the first time as I saw his look of concern. "You're deep in thought." And he looked over to the children embroiled in a massive game of British Bulldog, having roped in Turner among others. It was good to see him having fun. This was the last time we were going to be seeing him for a while.

I'd been spending more and more time with Turner – unintentionally. He'd started seeing a psychologist, talking through his problems. He'd taken to turning up at the stables whenever he had a spare moment, offering his help. I'd given him the odd job to do, but the more I gave him the more he wanted. I hadn't noticed at first, the gradual creep – but Trent had. "He's becoming overly attached to you," he'd told me. I hadn't seen it, but Turner, who'd booked himself into a residential centre for some intensive therapy, had.

"Are you all right?"

"More than." I smiled as he grinned at my response.

"Good. I was thinking it was about time we got going."

"Oh, I don't want to break up the party."

"We won't, they'll carry on long after we've left. Come on...it's time for our honeymoon to start, and I thought we might go and get on with some of that cherishing we both promised," he cajoled.

"Okay, shall we walk?"

"We'll take the car. We're not going to the stables."

Oh? My stomach plummeted. "Where are we going?" My small voice sounded as miserable as I suddenly felt.

"Can't tell you that, it's a surprise. It's only a couple of days, Emma, nothing grand. I thought you'd appreciate a break..." His voice tailed off, and I realised I needed to buck myself up. He wasn't to know how this would affect me, the worries I would have about being separated from Susie.

Forcing a smile, I replied as cheerily as I could, "No, Trent, that will be great...absolutely great. Don't I need to pack or something? I could pop back, throw a few things into a case..." I could at least say goodbye to her then.

"No need, it's already done. Everything's been taken care of."

"But what about Susie?" I had to ask.

"Everything's been taken care of," he repeated.

"Oh." I found myself looking for Greene, wondering if she knew what was going on.

"Emma...Emma," he repeated, dragging my attention back to him.

"Yes?"

"Do you trust me?"

"Yes."

"Then trust me...okay?"

"Okay," I sighed. I couldn't say any more. I knew he wouldn't understand. He leant over to kiss me, then held out his hand for mine, pulling me to my feet as he announced we were leaving.

Our friends lined the way as we kissed and hugged each one on our way to the front door, where the Jaguar waited for us. The door closed, and in no time at all we were leaving our cheering friends behind as we drove off, hearing the rattling sound of tins being dragged as they bounced and spun off the road behind us.

As soon as we were hidden by the trees we stopped, and Trent, after removing the tins, pulled a scarf out from behind his seat, folding it over. Then he held it up and leant towards me. I realised he was intending to blindfold me.

"Really?" I exclaimed as he grinned.

"It will heighten the suspense," he teased as he wrapped the scarf around my head and knotted it.

"Well it's a fine time to tell me you're into all that," I muttered, smiling as I heard him laugh. The engine revved and we set off again. The blindfold was immediately disorientating, although I knew when we were passing the stables, my heart reaching out as I thought of the sad little dog waiting inside for me to return. It was only a couple of days, I reasoned. I should enjoy the spontaneity, but the truth was I didn't. I just felt sick.

We travelled on, and I tried to imagine the road and where we might be going. I knew when we stopped at the main gate because I heard the gates opening and felt us driving through. I hoped we weren't going too far, and that no one would spot us and think I was being kidnapped and call the police. I wondered where our cases were, and what had been packed and would it be suitable for where we were going. Trent's hand came over and took mine, his thumb caressing the back of my hand, as soothing as his words.

"Stop stressing, Em, I can hear your worried thoughts from here. This is meant to be enjoyable." And I could hear the smile in his voice. Maybe it is for you, I thought, a little unkindly.

As soon as we drove through the gates I was lost. I could no longer imagine the road before us. With no idea of where we were going, I could do nothing but sit back and fret. However, only a couple of minutes had passed before Trent loosened his hand on mine and I heard the gears change down as we slowed, turning then carrying on again. A little later we slowed again, turned into somewhere and came to a stop. Okay then, I thought, not too far away, and reaching up I began to take off the blindfold.

"Don't," said Trent, and I stopped. Anticipation grew as Trent got out of the car and came round to my side. He opened the door and he took my hand as he helped me out. There was a slight give in the ground beneath me as I stood up. The car door closed, and Trent led me forward a few steps. The night air was cool on my skin. I felt him reach up to the blindfold. "Ready?" His breath whispered hot against my cheek.

He gently pulled off the scarf and I blinked. Cascades of white fairy lights hung around and in between the trees on each side of the path ahead. Threading his fingers through mine, Trent led me up the path to the foot of the steps that wound around the tree until they reached the tree house. More lights were wrapped around the banister as we climbed the stairs. I could see all the shutters had been folded back from the windows, and I paused before we got to the top as I looked at the door sporting the new addition of the cat flap. My face broke into an enormous smile. "You knew."

His head inclined slightly. "I knew...and you need to learn to trust me." There was a disturbance within – a scuffling noise followed by a rattle, and a scruffy, patchy head appeared through the catflap, followed by the rest of Susie as she wiggled her way towards us, squirming for attention as I knelt to give it to her.

Trent leaned forward to open the door, and as I joined him on the top step he scooped me up into his arms and carried me into the tree house, Susie jumping around his feet. Putting me down, he still held me close, one hand on my waist, one in my hair tilting my face to his as our lips met, tender and sweet, my fingers running through his hair. The kiss deepened into something more, our need growing as our tongues met, briefly, fleetingly, and I pulled away, knowing if I didn't we'd get no further than the kitchen, and that was not what I had planned for our wedding night.

Trent pushed the door closed, the room darkening to the level of light coming from the night sky as I said goodnight to Susie and she settled back into her bed. Then, taking my hand, he led me through to the bedroom. Opening the door, I gasped. The room was richly decorated in warm, comfortable colours, the bed dressed in deep crimson, with thick covers and plump pillows. More soft white fairy lights wound through the curlicues of the black ironwork of the bed, enough to give a glow to the room and nothing more. My picture of Eva sat on a small table next to the bed. The tops of the surrounding trees were silhouetted against a deep purple sky scattered with distant sparkles of light.

I turned to Trent as I nodded in understanding. "So this is the right time..."

"...For this place," he finished, his eyes never leaving mine as he kicked off his shoes, his socks following.

"You knew this...even then?"

"Even then." His jacket shrugged off, flung across a chair.

"Are you ever unsure about anything?"

"In matters concerning you?...No." He unbuttoned his waistcoat, taking it off to join the jacket. I hadn't moved and he now stepped closer, his hands reaching up to my shoulders. His thumbs easing the fabric over the curve of my shoulder as, with the barest movement from me, the dress fell, cascading down my body until it lay in a shimmering pool around my feet. I thanked Greene silently for being in charge of dressing me. I stood before him, high heels, stockings, suspenders, the briefest pair of pants I had ever owned and a plunging bra. I tried to look confident, feeling better when I saw his reaction - an exhaled breath of carnal appreciation.

He held out a hand to me and taking it, I stepped out of my dress and closer to where I could feel his heat, smell his scent. I kissed him softly, slowly, his tongue flicking across mine, teasing, tempting, and eager. Then ignoring his exhaled frustration I held him back from taking more as I unbuttoned his shirt, undid his cufflinks. My fingers trailing through the hair on his chest, then across his stomach, his skin soft over hard muscle, pulling his shirt out of his trousers then pushing it up, over his shoulders, and down his arms where it fell to the floor and moving closer I tasted his skin, my teeth grazing his nipple feeling his sharply inhaled breath as he stopped me.

Bringing my face to his he kissed me his arms closing around me as he unhooked my bra, letting it drop, his hands caressing my breasts followed by his lips, his tongue travelling across my body, licking, kissing, exploring, my

196

skin tingling as anticipation built. He dropped to his knees before me reaching to take off first one shoe then the other, unhooking my stockings then peeling them off one by one, rolling them down my legs and casting them aside. Reaching round he undid the suspender belt sending it in the same direction then finally, slipping his fingers under the strings that barely held my pants together, he drew them slowly down my legs lavishing attention on the flesh revealed, his tongue hot, lambent, and driving me crazy.

Burying my hands in his hair I pulled him back up, his lips meeting mine hard and hungry. Bringing my hands down to undo his trousers, I felt him ready for me, heard his deep, throaty groan, the sexiest sound in the world as I stroked him. His kisses harsher now, demanding, his breathing deep as he picked me up, carried me to the bed and threw me on to it.

Fixing me with his darkening gaze, he undressed, far too slowly, keeping me waiting as I craved his touch, then crawling across the bed and over me; his lips traced their way up my body until he reached my neck. He stretched out deliciously alongside me and I reached for him, his skin warm and smooth against mine, his lips running along the contours of my jaw, finding my mouth. He twisted over, pulling me on top. Then feeling his hardness against me and aching to have him inside, my back arched as I slowly took him in, revelling in the feeling I moaned as I slipped down on to him. I stopped for a moment, settling and luxuriating in the sensation, taking him deeper, feeling his hips hitch as he grew restless beneath me. Then I moved, slowly at first, feeling the whole length of him, then faster, harder, heat building, skin slick, as I felt him under me raw, powerful and wanting more as we drove against each other. Our pleasure peaking, almost unbearable in its intensity, then crashing over, like water breaching a dam, and left trembling in its wake I cried out in sweet relief as waves pulsated through me, and I clung to his body damp and shuddering in its own release as we held each other tight. Our breathing slowing, heartbeats steading as eventually I brought my face to his. His lips now soft and gentle.

I sat up a little, my hands on his chest as I looked down at him and smiled, his hands on my hips kept me in place, as his gaze trailed down my body. "I liked the lingerie."

"It had the desired effect."

"It was a great added extra...but I only need you to have that effect on me." Just as well, I thought, it really wasn't my style. He sat up, our bodies close as he bent his head to kiss my breast. His tongue flicking across my nipple focused my attention as his arms came round me again.

I hadn't had much sleep but woke to light at the windows, the hazy grey of early morning rather than day. Slipping from underneath the covers I went to the window, picking up his shirt and putting it on to look at the view. I heard the first bird calls responding to the start of a new day. Trees surrounded us, but as the ground fell away to one side I could see the roof of the Manor in the distance. Looking down, I watched three deer moving slowly, carefully below us, one leading, antlers held proudly.

I felt out of sorts. It wasn't unusual these days, and it was hardly surprising given the lack of sleep and the excesses of yesterday: too many nerves, too much food, too much drink. I leant up against the window, my bottom perched on the sill, looking back towards the bed as I watched my beautiful husband sleeping, relaxed and peaceful. His sheets had been pushed down, one arm was bent, his hand lying across his bare stomach, the other flung out towards where I'd been lying.

He'd done well yesterday. I knew he was a man of deep commitment who took vows and promises seriously, and I knew he would do everything he could to abide by those that he'd made to me. On the other hand I also knew of his desire to protect me, and yesterday these traits of his had been in direct opposition to each other. I'd been surprised that he'd told me anything of the conversation about the ballistics report, but to give him his due that was part of his new open and honest policy. However he hadn't told me everything in his equal need to protect, concerned that in the state I'd been in recently this would cause me more worry.

I thought back to the fragmented conversation I'd strained to hear. Carlton's "What does that mean?" Trent and Cavendish answering, almost speaking in unison, "It means there was someone else on the estate, someone unaccounted for." I'd known the purpose of the ballistics report was to match the bullets and casings found against the weapons used both by them and us. That had been done, but it seemed there was one anomaly: the man at the stables. I presumed they meant the man who had stepped out in front of us in an attempt to prevent us from leaving the yard; the man who had called out to the other group in the jeep; the man who had died in front of us, a bullet in his head. Everyone on the estate denied taking that shot, and now that had been proven. No one on our side had fired it, and it was unlikely one of them would have taken out one of their own. Conclusion – someone else had been on the estate that night, someone who had done this one thing and nothing more to assist either side; done this thing that allowed us to escape but had left no other tracks behind. Someone who was neither on our side nor on theirs? I pondered on who this guardian angel could be but could find no answer, and I vowed to speak to Cavendish about it. He must surely have an idea as to who would be watching over Grace and the children.

A shiver jolted me out of this train of thought and I realised I was cold. I went back to the bed, tossed aside his shirt and climbed in, cuddling up to Trent as he complained, "You're freezing."

199

"Then warm me up," I breathed, knowing that would get his attention.

"That'd be my pleasure." His arms, my safe place, drew me close as all other thoughts were banished from my mind.

# Acknowledgements

I'd like to say a huge thank you to Helen Hart and the team at SilverWood Books for their advice and skills in assisting me with copy editing, proofreading and new covers as I worked to polish this novel, and who have been unfailingly supportive and enthusiastic as this book has come together.

I had a wonderful team of beta-readers to help me on this novel, giving up their time to read through and provide very useful feedback on the first draft, so a big thank you to Katherine Matthews, Sarah Postins, Debra Cartledge, Andrew Moore, Kathy Sapsed and Claire Millington.

A special thank you goes to Claire Millington for going the extra mile in not only spotting a technical glitch in the plot but also for coming up with the solution. Her expert help with the RAF terminology has been invaluable and any errors remaining are mine and mine alone!

My thanks to Dave Holland of Deeho for his knowledge, for answering my constant questions, and dealing with my demands as he helped me with my website and assisted with my explorations into the wonderful world of social media.

Last, but of course by no means least, I am truly thankful to my close and extended family, my friends, both in the real world and those in the generous and incredibly talented bunch of fabulous writers and supporters I feel specially connected to online (you all know who you are!), and finally the wonderfully supportive community in which I am lucky enough to live. You have all encouraged me and thank you just doesn't seem enough.

# Contact details

Thank you for reading this far. I'm always interested to hear from readers with any feedback, thoughts or observations they are willing to make. If you'd like to get in touch, or you want to hear about what's coming next you can do so through my website at Georgia Rose Books where you will also have the opportunity to follow my blog. Alternatively you can email me at info@georgiarosebooks.com for a chat or to request to go on my mailing list; follow me on Twitter @GeorgiaRoseBook; find me on Facebook or 'like' The Grayson Trilogy Page on Facebook. I look forward to hearing from you.

Finally, if you have enjoyed reading this, please tell ~~someone~~ *everyone* you know and, whatever you think of it, if you are able to, would you please consider leaving a review? Of whatever rating! You might not think your opinion matters, but I can assure you it does. It helps the book gain visibility and it informs other readers whether or not to purchase it, so if you could take a minute or two to leave a few words on Amazon and/or Goodreads that would be hugely appreciated.

Now, if you're sitting there holding a beautiful paperback in your hand and you're thinking that request doesn't include me... well please think again. It doesn't matter how or where you bought your paperback Amazon and Goodreads will still accept a review from you.

Emma's story will conclude in *Thicker than Water*.

Thank you

Printed by Amazon Italia Logistica S.r.l.
Torrazza Piemonte (TO), Italy

11407034R00123